IS IT POSSIBLE?

STORIES FROM LOST HISTORY

Enjoy!

2021

Doug Ohman

Pioneer Photography & Services

Copyright © 2021 Doug Ohman

Library of Congress Cataloging Date: Library of Congress Control Number:
2021905875

ISBN: 978-1638482324

Printed in the United State of America

Design by Barb Lappi / Lappi Design

Proofreading by Krin Ohman & Susan Israelson

For further information, please contact
Doug Ohman
3525 Ensign Ave. N
New Hope, MN 55427

763-543-1049

www.pioneerphotography.com

Email: pioneerphotos@comcast.net

Contents

INTRODUCTION

Welcome to a world of discovery. If you are reading this introduction, I am willing to bet you are either interested in history, enjoy a good story, or both. For the past several years, I have discovered a historical world that in the past, I hadn't even considered — the history and stories we walk over every day. It is amazing to me what history has been lost under our feet. By recovering this history, I have learned much about everyday life in America. The relics and coins all tell a story of our past. I use a metal detector to actually find the items, but it is the research that I do that improves my odds for actually finding lost history and creating a plausible story. Where did people gather for social events such as picnic outings? Where did the circus set up near a small town? Is that the field where the baseball team played its games one hundred years ago? These types of questions and many others need to be asked when determining the best and most productive places to metal detect.

After the actual discovery of the item, the research of that piece begins. What is it? This is the first question I ask myself when I pull it from the ground. Most of the time I know what it is, but there are items that I find which I have no idea what they are. After cleaning the dirt away, the relic many times becomes easier to identify. If I still can't identify it, I may post a photo of it on-line and ask the public to help me. The next question, how did it get there? Does the item connect to the site where I found it, or is it somewhat random that it is there? What is the story? This is my favorite question to ask. Although the answer is almost always unanswerable, I enjoy creating a possible explanation or story for the piece.

The following chapters are about relics and items that I have dug from the ground and have historically identified accurately, but don't have the actual story. For these I have created a possible story. Each story has accurate historical context weaved with fictional content to create the story. Yes, I have made up the stories and I hope you enjoy this approach as much as I do. History explained through a story is what this book is all about. With every story, I included facts and a historical timeline with the hope that it will give you a clearer picture of the historical context for each piece. Enjoy!

DEDICATION

I want to dedicate this book to my parents, Donald and Dianne, who instilled in me a love of history and adventure. They served as missionaries when I was a young boy and always encouraged me and my siblings to explore the world around us.

IS IT POSSIBLE?

STORIES FROM LOST HISTORY

Doug Ohman

Barber Dimes

Indian Head Penny

Tokens

CHAPTER 1

Coins & Tokens

In the world of metal detecting the most desired find for hunters is an old coin. Unfortunately, you have to dig a lot of trash targets before finding that 100 year old treasure, but when you do discover an old coin, the feeling that comes over you when you look into the dirt and see a glimmer of silver, is pure excitement. Honestly, older coins are scarce, and most detectorists find their share of modern (clad) coins on a regular basis.

Where do all the coins come from you may ask? Consider that by various estimates, between 66 and 74 percent of the pennies produced by the U.S. Mint get into the hands of consumers and then vanish from circulation. Since the U.S. Mint produced $4.16 billion dollars' worth of pennies in 2014, that means that as much as $3.08 billion of them will end up dropped on the sidewalk, slipping between the couch cushions or landing wherever else misplaced coins end up.

Although old coins are fun to find, old trade tokens might even more desired by hunters, because they immediately tell a local story. Coins are impossible to trace back to a particular location, but a token can tell us about a business that operated in an area years ago. We still use tokens today for such things as amusements, car washes and pizza.

Token coins or trade tokens are coin-like objects used instead of coins. A key point of difference between a token coin and a legal tender coin is that the latter is issued by a governmental authority. Both can be freely exchanged for goods.

The Big Game

FACTS ▸ I found this 1942 German coin near Princeton, Minnesota, at an old one-room schoolhouse location. It was a cool day in March and the ground was partially frozen, but in the area that had direct sunlight the ground was soft enough to put a shovel in. When I first laid eyes on the coin, I thought it was a token, but then I saw the German lettering, eagle and most interesting the swastika, I knew it was a coin. It was a DEUTSCHES REICH 10 REICHSPFENNIG.

Not too far from the schoolhouse a World War II POW camp was located. This camp was opened in September of 1943 and was the first official Prisoner of War camp to open in Minnesota. Although the prisoners at this camp were Italian and not German, many of them had fought alongside the German army in the Tunisian campaign of North Africa. Could this coin have belonged to a prisoner who was captured and taken half way around the world to spend the remaining years of the war in Minnesota?

Luigi Esposito could smell New York City before he could see it through the fog, as he and his mother excitedly waited to be in America for the first time. Grandma and Grandpa would be waiting at the docks and were equally excited to see their daughter and their grandson. It had been many years since they waved goodbye to their daughter at the port in Naples, Italy. The grandparents were part of the mass immigration wave to America from Italy in the early 1920s. Now in 1934, they had established themselves as American citizens and were doing much better than they had in their home country.

Maybe the thing Luigi was looking forward to the most was a promise his grandfather had told him in a letter just a few weeks prior. That promise was to take him to a New York Yankee baseball game at the famous Yankee Stadium in the Bronx. After a few days of visiting, the exciting day finally came for young Luigi. They got to the stadium early to watch batting practice which included the famous players Babe Ruth and Lou Gehrig. Although years later Luigi couldn't even remember the score of the game or even who the Yankee's played that day. What he would remember though was that his love for American baseball started while sitting in the first base bleachers eating peanuts and drinking Coca-Cola with his grandpa.

Back home in Italy a month later, Luigi couldn't stop talking to his friends about America. Eventually the conversation always came back to baseball. Little did he know that he would be back in America in less than ten years, not to watch baseball, but as a prisoner of war. He had joined the Italian army in 1941 and was sent to North Africa to fight alongside German troops against the British and American forces. During the infamous Tunisian campaign, he was captured by the Americans and sent to the United States. This time he wasn't greeted at the docks in New York by his grandparents, but was quickly boarded on a train by armed guards for a long trip into the interior. During the train ride that lasted two days, Luigi spent most of his time looking

POW potato farm near Princeton

out the window amazed at the wide-open flat countryside that looked nothing like Italy. To pass the time, during the evenings, he played poker with some German prisoners.

The train finally stopped at a place the conductor called Camp Clark, Missouri. After spending a week living in rundown barracks the hundred or so prisoners were given blue denim uniforms with the letters "PW" on the back and then put back on a train heading north to Minnesota. The next day, Luigi was sitting by the window, and read the depot sign for Princeton. This is where the prisoners would call home for the next couple of months.

During their stay at a local potato/onion farm a few miles from town, the prisoners formed sports teams to pass the time. Most played soccer, but Luigi organized a baseball team. Lacking other teams in camp to play against, the baseball team received special permission to play some local town teams on Saturday afternoons. Luigi would always remember his best day on the diamond. They were playing a local team called the "Orrock Boys" at a small country schoolhouse field. Luigi played outfield, but it wasn't his play in the field that he would remember, but the hit he got to tie the game. His safe slide for a double kept the prisoners in the game until the ninth inning when the

boys from Orrock won the game with a home run ball that ran down the hill into the young pine trees behind the schoolhouse.

During that glorious slide to tie the game, Luigi lost the German 10 Pfennig coin he had won in one of those late night poker games on the train. He was keeping it for a good luck souvenir. Luigi eventually made his way back to Italy after the war, but would recall for the rest of his life, his time in Minnesota and that one glorious afternoon at a country school ball field.

HISTORICAL NOTE » By the end of World War II Minnesota had more than fifteen POW camps housing mainly German captives.

 1942

February 26 » The 14th Academy Awards ceremony is held in Los Angeles; How Green Was My Valley wins Best Picture.

June 4-7 » World War II – Battle of Midway: The United States Navy defeats an Imperial Japanese Navy attack against Midway Atoll.

October 28 » The Alaska Highway is completed.

December 1 » Gasoline rationing begins in the United States.

Wheat Pennies

Fall Festival

FACTS
While metal detecting behind the St. John's Catholic Church in the small Minnesota town of Darwin with my good friend Jay, I found this amazing Canadian coin. It was a 1 cent Queen Victoria. The coin was too worn to read a date; my best guess it was from the 1880s. The image of Queen Victoria verifies the later mint date. Canada produced two versions of this coin and this was of the latest version. Victoria was Queen of the United Kingdom of Great Britain and Ireland from June of 1837 until her death in May of 1876.

St. John's Catholic Church was started by Irish immigrants in the late 1870s. Could this coin have traveled from Canada by Irish settlers who came through Montreal in the later immigration period? On the coin itself it said, Dei Gratia Regina. This is Latin meaning "By the Grace of God, Queen".

Grace always loved a good party and the upcoming celebration at church was promising to be just what she was hoping for. Grace McKinney was only fifteen years old, but had already had her eye on a young man she had only met once at church earlier that spring. The only thing she knew about him was his name was Patrick and he lived near the neighboring town of Dassel. She prayed for weeks that this boy would be at the fall festival.

The church had been built in 1878, and now six years later was raising money for furnishing the new church. The fall festival was sure to bring in donations to finally get the basic things every Catholic Church needed, such as a bell for the tower, a main alter, and the complete set of Stations of the Cross.

The autumn day for the festival finally arrived and Grace got up early to do her Saturday chores. Her brothers milked the cows, and she tended to the chickens and the small herd of goats. When the chores were finished, she cleaned up for the festival and put on her new neatly pressed Sears and Roebuck dress. She always carried a few coins in her clutch purse to church just in case she felt the overriding guilt of the donation box. She secretly hoped today would be guilt free and she could spend some egg money on ice cream and maybe a colorful hair ribbon that one of the older ladies would have for sale.

Her father parked the family wagon next to the horse barns located behind the church. Grace couldn't wait to ditch her family and mingle with the other girls her age. Her group of friends had gathered near the half built stone grotto just east of the church. Most of the girls already had their ice cream cones in hand, so Grace had some catching up to do. In the haste to get her double scoop and meet up with her friends, she forgot to zip her purse closed and a couple of coins dropped into the tall grass of the church yard. She never missed the coins she lost,

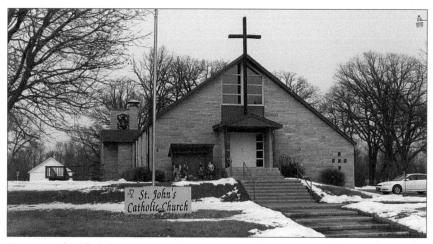

Current Church

maybe because she had other things on her mind. That afternoon when the festival was winding down her hope was realized and she got to share a soft drink with her new friend Patrick.

Grace would eventually marry the Irish boy from Dassel and they would remain members of St. John's for over fifty years. 🪙

HISTORICAL NOTE » Minnesota isn't even close to the top of the list for Irish emigration. That designation would go to eastern states like Massachusetts and New York. Minnesota is rightly known for German and Scandinavian heritage.

 TIMELINE ▷ 1906

February 26 » Upton Sinclair publishes The Jungle, a novel depicting the life of an immigrant family in Chicago during the early 1900s.

April 14 » Azusa Street Revival, an event which launches the Pentecostal movement in Christianity.

April 18 » The 1906 San Francisco earthquake on the San Andreas Fault destroys much of San Francisco, California.

September 24 » U.S. President Theodore Roosevelt proclaims Devils Tower, Wyoming as the nation's first National Monument.

Tokens

Presidential Token
Chester A. Arthur

Soap Token

Skipping School

Hunting in a small park in the Minneapolis suburb of Brooklyn Park, I found this amazing piece of history. I knew right away that it wasn't a coin. It was too lightweight, and after a quick clean I could see and feel it was aluminum. What surprised me was the date of 1934. Not too many years before this date, aluminum was considered one of the most valuable metals in the world. By the turn of the 19th/20th century, aluminum began to be used in many products including in the transportation industry for automobiles and early aircraft. Electricity allowed for cheaper extraction and the lightweight metal became its best attribute.

The token was produced by the Alcoa Aluminum Company as a sample of the material used to produce the new Union Pacific train that was built by the Pullman Car MFG Corp. The token was given out to those who attended the Chicago World's Fair in 1934. This was the second World's Fair that Chicago had hosted, and by the time it closed, it had been visited by nearly 40 million fairgoers.

Henry was excited to see his dad drive up the driveway that fall day in 1934. His dad would have the train tickets for the long awaited trip to Chicago for the World's Fair. Earlier that day at school, Henry told his 10th grade science teacher that he would write a detailed paper about what he saw and learned at the Century of Progress Exposition.

Henry loved science and hoped one day to become a scientist or an inventor. He wasn't sure what he looked forward to the most. Was it the train ride from Minneapolis? Was it the actual Exposition itself or was it a week off of school? Whatever it was, they were leaving in the morning.

The scenic train ride through southern Minnesota along the Mississippi River and the picture book scenery of Wisconsin dairy farms kept a smile on Henry's face for nearly 400 miles. They had reservations at the famous Drake Hotel on the north side of the city and on the nice days they would walk to Grant Park, the north entrance of the fair. Henry's father, always a good sport on these walks, would challenge Henry to foot races from block to block which helped to speed up the commute.

Henry was impressed by the crowds at the fair. He had seen large crowds in Minneapolis, but nothing like this. His Dad had taken him to see Governor Floyd B. Olson at a state capital event, but compared to these Chicago crowds, that seemed small.

On their second day at the Fair, Henry finally made it to the Hall of Science building and the Travel and Transport Exhibits. He spent hours looking at the new automobile prototypes being introduced by Ford and General Motors. He loved the Union Pacific exhibit which was showcasing their new aluminum made streamline engine and passenger cars. It was at this exhibit that he was handed a lightweight token souvenir before taking a 20 minute tour of the train. It wasn't until later that evening back at the hotel that he

looked closer at the token. It said "Lucky Piece" and sure enough, he felt it.

The trip ended on Friday, but on a high note with tickets for bleacher seats at the famous Soldier Field Stadium to hear an address given by President Franklin Roosevelt. Later that day, Henry began to write the promised science paper as the train took him and his dad back to Minnesota. He had just experienced the trip of a lifetime and was excited to share it with his friends and classmates.

Years later, Henry didn't remember what happened to the "Lucky Piece" aluminum token, but it was lost. What he would remember for the rest of his life was that memorable September week with his dad in 1934.

HISTORICAL NOTE » A Century of Progress was organized as an Illinois nonprofit corporation in January 1928 for the purpose of planning and hosting a World's Fair in Chicago in 1934. City officials designated three and a half miles of newly reclaimed land along the shore of Lake Michigan between 12th and 39th streets on the Near South Side for the fairgrounds. Held on 427 acres , the $37,500,000 exposition was formally opened on May 27, 1933, by US Postmaster General James Farley at a four hour ceremony at Soldier Field.

TIMELINE 1934

January 26 » The Apollo Theater opens in Harlem, New York City.

May 16 » Teamsters in Minneapolis begin a strike that lasts until a settlement proposal is accepted on August 21.

June 15 » Great Smoky Mountains National Park is established.

August 19 » The first All-American Soap Box Derby is held in Dayton, Ohio.

Happy Reunion

FACTS I first thought it was an old dime. Looking closer I was excited when I realized I had found an old trade token. I had been metal detecting on an old farm site in what is today the city of Brooklyn Park. Early plat maps and a 1938 aerial photo clearly showed a farm at the site. After cleaning up the token the front revealed the name "Ingebretsen & Ahlm" and the back had a date of 1909. Getting home later that night, I began to research the token. It came from a grocery store that was located in the Cedar-Riverside area of Minneapolis.

Cedar-Riverside, a neighborhood just east of downtown Minneapolis, has been a major entry-point for newcomers to Minnesota for over 160 years. In the 1850s, the area attracted migrants from New England and the Mid-Atlantic States. Over the next fifty years they were joined by waves of immigrants in search of new opportunities - Norwegians, Danes, Swedes, Finns, Irish, Germans, Slovaks, Czechs, Poles, Swiss, Canadians, French and many others. These newcomers helped build Minneapolis. They ran businesses and worked in construction, in domestic service, in the millinery trade and in the lumber, milling and brewing industries. In 1910, the Cedar-Riverside population peaked to nearly 20,000. Over fifty percent were Scandinavian and the neighborhood became a cultural center for Scandinavian communities in Minneapolis.

Charles Ingebretsen Sr. emigrated from Norway in the early 1900s, the only member of his family to leave the country. He went to Fargo, North Dakota and learned butchering. He then came to the Twin Cities where the Scandinavian-American community was flourishing in the Cedar-Riverside neighborhood. His first business was at 1808 Riverside, a location close to both the Southern Theater, which had entertainment for Scandinavian immigrants and the railroad switchyards, which employed many Norwegians, Swedes, and Danes. He soon expanded the business, opening several other meat markets and grocery stores serving other Scandinavian communities, including the Model Meat Market on East Lake St., strategically located on a streetcar line.

Kristina Lindberg couldn't wait for her sister Anna to arrive in Minneapolis from Sweden. It had been nearly five years since she had seen her younger sister. Kristina was sure that Anna was all grown up and would have no trouble fitting into the fast-paced life of America. Back on the farm in Sweden, Anna had taken care of their folks until just a few weeks ago when both parents passed away during a flu epidemic that swept through the village and country side in Smaland. Even though the flu affected the United States in a harsh way, Anna was willing to take the risk of travel to be with her older sister.

Kristina waited patiently at the Milwaukee Road depot for the train from Chicago which she hoped Anna was on. The smoke from

the many trains and the bustling noise of hundreds of passengers began to make Kristina anxious. Would Anna even recognize her? Or more importantly, would she remember what Anna even looked like after so long? Her fears were quickly gone when right on time, the 2:30 PM train pulled into the station and her sister was one of the first to step down on the main platform. Kristina magically switched languages from English to Swedish as the two sisters hugged and cried in excitement. Kristina had many questions to ask Anna as they rode the street car from downtown to her neighborhood near the University of Minnesota. They got off at a local grocery store three blocks from Kristina's house to pick up some special treats for their first dinner together. Ingebretsen's was Kristina's favorite store because it always had the freshest produce and the tastiest herring all year long. Anna insisted on paying for the food, but Kristina told her that she had some store credit saved up in tokens that she could use. They argued but eventually the older sister won out. Getting just enough food that they could carry in their arms they dragged Anna's trunk down the sidewalk giggling all the way to Kristina's house.

In time, both Kristina and Anna would marry. Kristina met a local farmer who had bought some land out west of Minneapolis near Robbinsdale where they would be potato farmers for over forty years. Anna stayed in Minneapolis where she and her college professor husband raised eight children. 🪙

 1910

February 8 » The Boy Scouts of America youth organization is incorporated

May 11 » The U.S. Congress establishes Glacier National Park in Montana.

June 19 » The first unofficial Father's Day is observed.

July 24 » James MacGillivray publishes the first account of Paul Bunyan in the Detroit News.

Paying Tribute

FACTS I had just purchased my first metal detector and was excited to find treasure. In a wooded area outside an old abandoned cemetery site, I got a faint signal that I thought I should dig. Five inches down I pulled out this Shield nickel. I had never seen one and didn't know at the time what I had found. My excitement only grew when after rubbing the coin on my jeans; I was able to make out a date of 1869 and "United States of America". Unfortunately, I nicked the coin with my digging shovel. As of this writing, this is the second oldest coin I have found.

The Shield nickel was the first United States five-cent piece produced out of copper-nickel, the same alloy of which American nickels are struck today. Designed by James Longacre, the coin was issued from 1866 until 1883, when it was replaced by the Liberty Head nickel. The coin takes its name from the motif on its obverse, and was the first five-cent coin referred to as a "nickel" - silver pieces of that denomination had been known as half dimes.

Timothy was excited to vote in the presidential election that year. His hero was running as the Republican candidate and was sure to win the state of Minnesota. Even though the Civil War had been over for nearly four years, Ulysses S. Grant was the most popular figure in America.

In 1863, Timothy had fought with the 5th Minnesota Regiment and would never forget seeing General Grant ride to the front lines to check on the troops in the battle of Vicksburg. The men on both sides actually stopped fighting in order to catch a glimpse of the General. This image of General Grant on his horse would be seared into Timothy's memory for the rest of his life.

Back home on the farm in Minnesota, Timothy kept up with state and national politics through reading the local newspapers and attending political speeches in both St. Anthony and St. Paul. When the candidates were announced for the 1868 election, Timothy had no doubt who would win by a landslide.

Four years later, President Grant completed a round the world tour and was scheduled to be in the Midwest later that fall. Timothy convinced his wife to let him take the train to Dubuque to see the President as a way to honor his war buddies. The fall harvest had been good that year and she agreed that Timothy deserved a short vacation to see his war hero. Before leaving for Iowa, Timothy visited the two graves of his war comrades who were buried in a small cemetery near his farm. Both of his buddies had died shortly after the war. One from a leg wound suffered in the battle of Nashville and the other died in a farming accident after returning home. Timothy sat near the two graves remembering those war years as if they happened yesterday. He even caught himself talking to his buddies telling them that he was going to see the General. Before leaving the cemetery, Timothy did what he had always done; he left some coins on their markers. It was tradition to leave coins in honor of one's war buddies.

Later that week Timothy did see the President, but the crowds were so large that he couldn't get close enough to actually hear the speeches. On the return trip back to Minnesota, Timothy had more time to reflect

and thought he would try to visit as many of the 5th Minnesota boys that were in the area. If there was enough interest, he would start a Grand Army of the Republic post. ⊙

HISTORICAL NOTE » Leaving a penny at the grave means simply that you visited. A nickel indicates that you and the deceased trained together, while a dime means you served with him in some capacity. By leaving a quarter at the grave, you are telling the family that you were with the soldier when he or she was killed.

 1868

February 24 » Impeachment of Andrew Johnson, President of the United States.

May 30 » Memorial Day is observed in the United States for the first time.

July 5 » Preacher William Booth establishes the Christian Mission, predecessor of The Salvation Army.

October 28 » Thomas Edison applies for his first patent, the electric vote recorder.

Coin of Remembrance

FACTS Sometimes in metal detecting you find things in the strangest places and that was the case when I found this beautiful 1944 silver half dollar. My bother Dan and I were out in the woods along the banks of the Rum River north of Milaca, Minnesota. Early in the hunt, I received a good strong signal through my headphones that stopped me my tracks. Of all the coins I have pulled from the ground, this coin was in the very best condition. The coin looked like it was just dropped yesterday. You might expect to find a coin like this on a historic property, but not deep in the woods along the river.

The Walking Liberty half dollar is a silver 50-cent piece or half dollar coin that was issued by the United States Mint from 1916 to 1947; it was designed by Adolph A. Weinman, a well-known sculptor and engraver.

The design of the half dollar bears a full-length figure of Liberty, the folds of the Stars and Stripes flying to the breeze as a background, progressing in full stride toward the dawn of a new day, carrying branches of laurel and oak, symbolical of civil and military glory. The hand of the figure is outstretched in bestowal of the spirit of liberty. The reverse of the half dollar shows an eagle perched high upon a mountain crag, his wings unfolded, fearless in spirit and conscious of his power. Springing from a rift in the rock is a sapling of mountain pine, symbolical of America.

Front   Back

Deer hunting weekend was almost as important as Christmas in the Peterson family. Relatives from as far away as South Dakota and Illinois would make the trip to Milaca for the annual hunt. John and Gloria didn't have a big house, but if the guys wouldn't mind bunking in the barn, the women would make do in the three upstairs bedrooms while the kids took over the living room. On Friday, before the big day the guys cleaned and checked their guns, bragged about the past hunts and drank their share of beer, while the women prepared the traditional chili and corn bread for Sunday. This year 1946, had an extra sense of excitement, for it was the first hunt they had since 1941. The war had interrupted a forty year Peterson tradition.

This year also brought a bit of sadness as well. Benjamin Peterson would have been twenty-two years old. Sadly, Benjamin's platoon was one of the first to try to land on the beaches of Okinawa. According to the letter from the War Department, John and Gloria were told that Benjamin never even got out of the landing craft before it hit an underwater mine.

On the last hunt in 1941, Benjamin, just seventeen, had shot the largest buck anyone in the family could remember. From his deer stand along the old Tote road leading from Milaca to Onamia, Benjamin got his trophy deer. The younger guys gave Benjamin a hard time because they said he picked the best spot for himself along a well-known trail and clearing to the Rum River.

The morning of this year's hunt all the men gathered in the barn for a moment of silence to remember Benjamin. The day could not have been more perfect. A light snow had fallen during the night and the day promised to be ideal with little wind and bright sunshine. They all agreed to leave their stands at ten o'clock and meet at Benjamin's old tree stand. If they hadn't filled out their tags by then, they would organize some deer drives to finish the day.

It was a little unnerving for some of the guys to look up the tree and still see the well-built platform of Benjamin's old deer stand. The wooden 2 x 4 ladder steps nailed into the tree were still firmly in place. It was just then that Roger Peterson, Benjamin's uncle, suggested "Why don't each of us climb the tree ladder and leave a token of remembrance for Ben." Some left rifle shells, some their old hunting caps and others left coins.

‖‖ TIMELINE ▷ 1946

July 4 » The Philippines is granted independence by the United States.

September 22 » Yogi Berra makes his Major League Baseball debut.

October 16 » The United Nations' first meeting in Long Island is held.

December 20 » Frank Capra's It's a Wonderful Life, featuring James Stewart, is released in New York.

The Big Storm

Front

Back

I have been asked, what do you like finding more; coins or tokens? I do like finding old coins, but it's hard to trace a coins history and tie it to a particular place. On the other hand, a token can often be connected to a place such as a town or business.

I get excited when I get permission to metal detect a historic property. My friend Mary Ostby is the director of the Benton County Historical Society. She recently told me that the Historical Society had purchased an old house in Sauk Rapids. The house was built in 1874 and the hope is to make it into a museum. I asked her if I could do some detecting in the yard and she thought that would be a great idea. I always offer whatever I find to the property owners and in this case I thought, if I find some local history, maybe a small display in the museum would be the result.

I spent about five hours metal detecting the yard and found some interesting old items. The best find of the day was this Brunswick pool token from a local bar in town. Doing further research, I discovered that the token dates to about 1885.

Brunswick Corporation, formerly known as the Brunswick-Balke-Collender Company, is an American corporation that has been developing, manufacturing and marketing a wide variety of products since 1845. Originally J. M. Brunswick intended his company to be mainly in the business of making carriages, but soon after opening his machine shop, he became fascinated with billiards, decided that making billiard tables would be more lucrative, as the better tables then in use in the United States were imported from England. Brunswick billiard tables were a commercial success, and the business expanded and opened the first of what would become many branch offices in Chicago, Illinois, in 1848. For many years the company's slogan was: "The oldest and most extensive billiard table manufacturers in the United States."

Pool or billiards has been around for a long time. Once a game mostly for the rich, the pool has become a mainstay feature in bars, resorts, playrooms, and homes of individuals from all walks of life. Although the initial history of the game is still unknown, it is believed that billiards has been executed in many ways for quite a while. Originally played as a lawn sport, the most current variations of billiards are widely recognized as French versions of traditional billiard games. Pocket Billiards is the game traditionally played in the USA and Canada. There are also a lot of variations of the pool, including nine balls and eight balls and many others.

Although the specific origin of this game is not well known, it is widely believed that the oldest and best-known types of billiards began in France in the fifteenth century. In the earlier days, Billiards enjoyed an incredible success mentioned in Shakespearean plays and appreciated by celebrities, scientists, and politicians for instance; Napoleon, Mozart, and George Washington were among the most acclaimed and enthusiasts of the game.

Roy Stanton had several investment options to pick from. Businesses were growing fast in the river town of Sauk Rapids, but there was one investment that Roy considered near the top of his list. Frank & Wayne Paulson, local businessmen, had recently purchased a rundown building on Benton Avenue and were looking for financial investors to help get a saloon up and running. The local Sauk Rapids Harald newspaper wrote: "What Sauk Rapids needs is a place where a man can go to for a stiff drink after a hard day's work." The nearest watering hole was three miles away in St. Cloud unless you were going north; then you had to wait until you arrived in Royalton.

Roy and his wife Abigail had arrived in Sauk Rapids two years before in the summer of 1883. Roy was the president of the local

bank and Abigail organized the local reading club. Her club met every Friday in the living room of their large home on 2nd street. Many of the women who attended the club lived in this upscale neighborhood, but Abigail's home was the nicest. The house was built of brick that was whitewashed to a glistening white that made a statement of wealth.

The Saloon opened in the spring of 1885. Roy along with other town men who did not support temperance were all present for the grand opening. The official ribbon cutting took place on the front steps. This was followed by a round of drinks and a group photo taken by a traveling photographer on his way through town.

Business at the F. & W. Saloon was strong through that first winter mainly due to the new Brunswick billiard table Frank had insisted on buying. On the other hand Wayne thought it was too expensive, but relented to the purchase if Frank would agree to charge patrons to play. After some back and forth, they agreed to charge five cents for a game of eight ball. The Brunswick salesman told the brothers that he would provide playing tokens in appreciation for them buying the table. Soon the tokens became a popular exchange for not only pool games, but for food and drink at the bar as well.

Roy arrived at the saloon at around 3:00 PM that April day. He would remember this day for the rest of his life. The weather had been unseasonably warm that entire spring, but this day just seemed different. After a quick drink, he challenged three of his business friends to a game of pool. Losing team had to pay. Roy felt lucky that day and he and his friend Stanley Olson won the game easily. The game was just finishing when a man ran into the saloon yelling something about the weather. Roy looked outside and couldn't believe how dark the sky looked for the middle of the day. A storm was clearly coming and Roy knew that he should head home just in case it got worse.

Abigail noticed the storm as well and began closing the windows of the house. She remembered seeing Roy running down 2nd street toward home as if he was being chased. Roy hadn't even made it to the front door when the cyclone hit. He flattened himself to the ground and began to pray. Abigail frantically went into the basement cellar hoping that Roy would soon follow. Roy never did make it into the house due to the strong wind. He laid in the yard for nearly an hour, too scared to stand up. All the windows of the house were shattered, but the house was intact. As it turned out both Roy and Abigail made it through that historic April 14th storm and would tell their grandchildren the incredible story of survival for years to come.

HISTORICAL NOTE » On April 14, 1886 at approximately 4:00 PM a cyclone struck the town of Sauk Rapids. Everything in the path of the tornado was demolished. It swept through the heart of the city, wiping out all the stores. In Sauk Rapids alone, forty-four were killed and several hundred injured.

 # 1886

February 14 » The first train load of oranges leaves Los Angeles via the transcontinental railroad.

June 2 » U.S. President Grover Cleveland marries Frances Folsom in the White House, becoming the only president to wed in the executive mansion. She is 27 years his junior.

September 4 » Indian Wars: After almost 30 years of fighting, Apache leader Geronimo surrenders with his last band of warriors.

October 28 » In New York Harbor, U.S. President Grover Cleveland dedicates the Statue of Liberty.

Indian Head Penny

1860 Indian Head Penny »
My oldest coin (so far)

Serving Others

FACTS Sometimes I find things metal detecting that completely surprise me. That was the case when I found this foreign silver coin in a small park in Coon Rapids. Why was it there and how did it become lost? I never tire of these questions. This find is a great example of why I love the hobby of metal detecting. Each day you go out, you never know what history you will discover.

The rupee is the official currency of India. The history of the India rupee traces back to Ancient India in circa 6th century BCE, ancient India was one of the earliest issuers of coins in the world. From 1858 through 1947 the British Crown ruled India.

After the death of King George V in 1936, his son, King Edward VIII became king, but abdicated before the coronation. No coins were minted using his portrait. His younger brother the Duke of York was crowned as King George VI in May of 1937 and the first coin of India with his effigy was minted in 1938.

Ronald liked Sunday school especially when the church would have a missionary speaker and all the kids were allowed to sit with the adults upstairs in the main sanctuary to see the slide show and hear about foreign lands. It might have been in one of those services that Ronald decided that someday he would become a missionary himself.

Ronald's mother never allowed him, and his brothers and sisters to ever miss going to church. Even when the weather or the Polio epidemic should have kept them home, church was never cancelled. She would always remind the children, "kids in foreign lands live in conditions a lot worse than us and would love to be able to go to church every week."

The call to become a missionary never waned with Ronald. After high school in the fall of 1947 he enrolled as a freshman at North Central Bible College in Minneapolis. At first his class schedule required all the basic courses, but by the time he was a junior, two years later, he was taking many of the school's mission courses. All he could think about at that time was graduating, marrying his sweetheart, Esther, and fulfilling his missionary call.

That call came just weeks after commencement. A local church that Ronald was attending made a decision to send Ronald and his bride to help an older missionary couple serving in Bombay, India. The goal was to eventually take over the India mission and if it be God's will, expand it to nearby towns and villages.

Ronald and Esther served for seven years in India. Their time on the mission field was good for the most part, but after having four kids, Esther's health began to suffer. Coming back to the States wasn't easy for Ronald, but he knew it would be best for Esther. At first they lived with Ronald's folks in Minneapolis, but soon took advantage of an affordable housing option in the expanding suburb of Coon Rapids. A builder by the name of Orrin Thompson was developing entire neighborhoods with his sturdy 3 bedroom ramblers.

« Mexican Centavos

Buffalo Nickel »

"This will be perfect," Ronald told Esther. As it turned out it, they did pick the perfect location across the street from a soon to be developed park. Ronald spent hours at the park teaching his kids baseball, riding bikes and having family picnics.

Every summer Ronald and Esther, working with their local church, helped organize "Missions in the Park". The event was an outreach ministry and Ronald always set up a display booth with many of the souvenirs, trinkets and clothing they had brought home from their time in India. His booth was always popular especially with the kids in the neighborhood because he always served ice cream cones along with giving away a free pocket size New Testament.

Ronald and Esther have both passed away now, but their kids and grandkids still live in the area and occasionally, drive by the house and the park that hold so many memories. 🌑

TIMELINE ⟩ 1944

June 6 » World War II – Battle of Normandy: Operation Overlord, commonly known as D-Day.

July 19 » President Franklin D. Roosevelt is renominated for a fourth term at the 1944 Democratic National Convention.

August 7 » IBM dedicates the first program-controlled computer.

August 9 » The United States Forest Service and the Wartime Advertising Council release posters featuring Smokey Bear for the first time.

Coins » My Favorites

Axel Hub Cap

Horseshoe

CHAPTER 2

Transportation

I t isn't long before everyone that puts the time into this hobby of metal detecting will discover some transportation relics. It might be a valve stem from a Model T or a horse buckle, but whatever it is, most detectorist love finding these types of treasures.

License Plate Topper

Crotal Bells

My favorite transportation relics are Crotal bells.
Crotal bells, also known as rumble bells, were used on
horse-drawn vehicles before motorized vehicles were
common. They were often made of bronze with a slot
cut down the side. These bells were used to warn other
horse-drawn vehicle users that another vehicle was
approaching. They came in many sizes, from a small
1-inch version to bells that were many inches across
— the older ones were forged while others were cast.
They were either hung on a small leather-and-iron
harness bracket above the horse's collar on smaller
vehicles. On larger vehicles, such as delivery wagons,
they were driven into the wooden frame of the wagon.

Coin Flip

FACTS One spring day I stopped at an old farm site just north of the Anoka High school to get permission to metal detect. To my surprise the current owner was a classmate of mine through grade school and junior high. After catching up after so many years, John gave me permission to check his yard with my detector. I didn't detect that day, but returned a few days later with my brother Dan. He used the detector and I dug the holes. We found a few modern coins, some scrap metal and then he got a signal that sounded great. The first photo shows the license a few minutes out of the ground and the second is what it looks like all cleaned and shined for the display in the Edina Historical Society museum.

A Morningside bike license badge would have been attached to the front frame of a bicycle. Both Dan and I thought we had heard of the town Morningside, but weren't sure. Morningside is an old streetcar suburb adjoining the Linden Hills neighborhood of the city of Minneapolis. Morningside is situated along the old Como-Harriet Streetcar Line and developed more quickly than the mostly rural village of Edina. In 1920, Morningsiders voted to secede from Edina and form their own village. Morningside remained a separate village for 46 years, until 1966, when, in response to state prompting, was reincorporated into the larger City of Edina.

Gail and her sister Cindy got along pretty well for being so close in age. The one thing though they did argue about almost on a regular basis, was about the bicycle they had to share. When Gail wanted to ride it, it seemed to be Cindy's turn and the same was true when it was Gail's turn, Cindy begged to ride.

As the warm summer of 1955 went into the Dog Days of August, the bike battle heated up as well. Their Dad finally agreed to look in the want ads of the Anoka Shopper newspaper for a second bike for the girls. Looking for three weeks straight, he had no luck finding a girls bike that would be a good fit. One day over his lunch break at Federal Cartridge, the local munitions factory in town, a friend of his on the assembly line mentioned that his oldest girl was going overseas with the Peace Corp and had a bicycle for sale. If Bill was interested, he would bring the bike to work the next day. Bills friend lived in Edina and thought his daughter's bike might be just what Bill was looking for.

When Gail and Cindy saw the bike for the first time, of course they both wanted it. With a flip of a coin, Gail won fair and square. She loved her new bike with only one exception. It was licensed to a town she had never heard of and knew that when her school friends would come out to the farm they would ask about it and tease her. She asked her dad to remove it and that was the last time she remembered ever seeing it. ✹

TIMELINE ▷ 1955

January 7 » Marian Anderson is the first African-American singer to perform at the Metropolitan Opera in New York City.

July 17 » The Disneyland theme park opens in Anaheim, California.

September 10 » Western series Gunsmoke debuts on the CBS television network.

December 15 » Johnny Cash's "Folsom Prison Blues", recorded on July 30, is released by Sun Records.

Big Responsibility

MINNESOTA TERRITORIAL CENTENNIAL 1849 – 1949

RED RIVER OX CART

3¢ UNITED STATES POSTAGE 3¢

FACTS This relic is one of the oldest treasures I have found so far in my hobby of metal detecting. It is an old oxen shoe that might date to as early as the 1840s. I can't say for certain on the date, but where I found it might give an idea of its age.

I was metal detecting only a few yards from East River Road in NE Minneapolis. This road followed the historic Red River Ox Cart Trail along the Mississippi River. The trail was known locally as the "Woods Trail".

In the early days of Minnesota settlement there developed an extensive trading enterprise from the Red River Valley to St. Paul. The best and most efficient way to move products in both directions was to use large two wheel carts pulled by oxen. The Red River

Banfill Tavern

cart was made entirely of wood. The cart was suspended between two large wheels, each more than five feet in diameter. The wheels had spokes that angled outward from the hubs to the rim, which helped stabilize the cart. The wheels could be taken off and lashed together and used as a raft to cross water. When they were used on land, their squeal could be heard from miles away because they could not be greased; grease would mix with the trail dust and either stop the wheels from turning or wear down the axel. The axel supported the cart's weight and, even without grease, wore out quickly. Travelers carried spare axels on their journeys; a typical trip from Winnipeg to St. Paul would require four or five.

Drivers used harnesses to hitch their carts to a horse or ox, whose head went through a collar. They attached the collar to the cart's shaft with leather straps called tugs. Usually, the cart was pulled by one animal, but there are some records of carts being pulled by two. Horses were first used, then oxen, which could pull up to 1,000 pounds.

Jonathan Smith could hear the carts coming down the trail well before seeing them. The cart caravan would be at the tavern within the hour. Jonathan hurried to have the tables set and the food and beer ready to serve. That morning Mr. Banfill left Jonathan in charge of the hotel and tavern as he left for St. Paul to attend the 1st Minnesota Legislature. Running the tavern would be a big responsibility, but Jonathan thought he was up for the task if only he had more help.

The cart caravan was the largest Jonathan had ever seen. Questions raced through his mind. Would there be enough food to serve the men? The long days on the trail always made men eat more than normal. What about the stable accommodations for the oxen? He didn't have enough so most of the oxen would have to stay outside. Mr. Banfill had instructed Jonathan not to worry, for his tavern was the last stop for the caravan before arriving the next day in St. Paul and the Teamsters would not ask too much of him. They would be tired but would leave early the next day for their last day on the trail. The only thing Mr. Banfill warned Jonathan about was that many of the oxen would need new shoes before arriving on the hard cobblestone streets of St. Paul. "Have our local blacksmith, Mr. Fisher ready," was the last thing Jonathan remembered hearing Mr. Banfill say.

The next morning the Teamsters were up early, but most didn't want the farrier services of Mr. Fisher. They just wanted to make sure they left quickly to make the last 20 miles to St. Paul before nightfall. Looking at the condition of the oxen and their shoes that morning, Mr. Fisher knew that without some repair work, some of the oxen would arrive in St. Paul in rough shape. As it turned out, several oxen lost their shoes before even making it to the falls of St. Anthony. *U*

HISTORICAL NOTE » The Banfill Tavern was built in 1847 by John Banfill, the building initially served as an inn and a base for logging operations northwest of Saint Anthony Falls. Due to its proximity to Minnesota's first Territorial Road and the Red River Trails, the inn became a popular rest stop for travelers. John Banfill was elected to the Minnesota State Senate for the 1st Minnesota Legislature in 1848.

May 29 » Sojourner Truth delivers the first version of her "Ain't I a Woman?" speech, at the Women's Rights Convention in Akron, Ohio.

September 18 » The New York Times is founded.

November 14 » Herman Melville's novel Moby-Dick; or The Whale is published in the U.S. by Harper & Brothers, New York.

December 2 » Stephen Foster's minstrel song "Old Folks at Home" is first published.

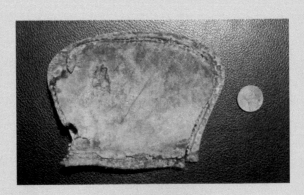

Horse
Blinder

Favorite Season

FACTS When I find a relic metal detecting that has writing on it, I know that there is a good chance I can do further research to find the story. That was the case in a Northeast Minneapolis park. I pulled out this broken pocket knife that was several inches underground. At first I didn't know what I had found. Doing research later at home revealed a very interesting automotive story.

This pocket knife was given away by automobile service stations to promote that they had the new innovated lift system. It was the first hydraulic lift that rotated the car 360 degrees, allowing cars to be driven in and out of the bay in a forward gear. It was developed by the Rotary Lift Company in Memphis Tennessee in 1925. Before this time, most service stations had a large pit that a car parked over as the mechanic worked from underneath.

Buying a car was all Robert could think about during the summer of 1940. He just had to have his own wheels before his senior year at Edison High school. His dad had helped him get a job on a framing crew that was building houses in the fast growing suburb of Columbia Heights. Although Robert was big for his age, he had no carpenter experience which made him the gopher on the crew. He was constantly being ordered around to get this and that. There were many days that summer that Robert wanted so badly to tell his boss off, but he knew that September was coming and the two things he wanted most would be his if he could just hang in there. Dreaming of his own car and playing football for Edison kept Robert on the miserable job all summer.

By the end of the summer, Robert had saved seventy five dollars and was ready to do some car shopping. His dad was a fireman working out of the Johnson street firehouse and knew a guy from work that had a used Studebaker for sale. Although the car had some dings and rust in the body, it seemed perfect to Robert and the price was right.

Robert learned from watching his dad take care of the family Buick that oil changes on a regular schedule could add years to the life of a car. The family mechanic was his uncle Melvin who had a shop down the hill on Lowry Avenue. As long as Robert could remember, he would go with his dad to the shop and watch his uncle change tires, oil or anything else that was needed on the Buick. As a kid his favorite memory from those visits to the shop was that his uncle would always buy him a root beer from the bottle machine.

Today would be different; Robert wouldn't be with his dad, but driving his own car to have it checked out by his uncle. "Is that new?" he asked his uncle who was lifting the Studebaker up in the air with a push of a lever. "Yes" his uncle said. "It's called a hydraulic lift. I had it installed last week by an outfit from Tennessee. It not only lifts the car, but rotates it as well."

The Studebaker checked out fine. "Make sure you bring her in for regular maintenance" his uncle said. As Robert was leaving his uncle gave him a small black pocket knife and told him that the company from Tennessee left a small box of these knives as a promotional advertisement. "Here take two or three to give to your buddies." Robert thanked his uncle and headed for Jackson Park where he was meeting some friends for a Saturday afternoon pickup game of touch football.

The following Monday would be the first day of his senior year and the start of the high school football season. Everything had worked out. First the summer job, then the car, and now his favorite season, football season. ◉

HISTORICAL NOTE » Automobile Rotary Lift Co. was started in 1925 by two oil men named R.J. O'Brien from Shreveport, LA and B.B. Jones from Jackson, MS under the Tennessee laws to build automobile lifts for service motor vehicles. In 1937, they were able to perfect and create the modern-day hydraulic elevator. They called them "Oildraulic" elevators. Elevators between 1925 and 1955 were installed using the "Rotary Co." name.

Tire Gauge

TIMELINE ▷ 1940

February 20 » Tom and Jerry make their debut in Puss Gets the Boot.

April 7 » Booker T. Washington becomes the first African American to be depicted on a United States postage stamp.

June 16 » The Sturgis Motorcycle Rally is held for the first time in Sturgis, South Dakota.

June 22 » The first Dairy Queen opens in Edina, Minnesota.

1924 Minnesota License Plate

My Partner Jack

One of my favorite things to search for in metal detecting is bridle rosettes, also known as bridle buttons. A bridle rosette is a utilitarian accessory used on the harness of a horse. They are used in pairs to help position a bridle correctly on the animal's head.

Bridle buttons have a long history. They have probably been used for nearly as long as the bridles they have decorated. According to legend, superstitious people in ancient Egypt reportedly designed very early buttons as protection for their horses, with the rosettes supposedly attracting and neutralizing the "eyes" of evil spirits.

Bridle rosettes can run the full range from very plain to highly artistic. During the 1800s, they grew popular with the riding and driving public and were produced in increasingly decorative styles. By the Victorian period, thick glass domes were covering polished brass backs. Beneath the domes, fancy, colorful die cuts and transfers would be inserted. Flowers and animals were popular subjects.

I found this Modern Woodmen of America rosette on a curb strip in a small town in central Minnesota. Immediately I knew it was a rosette, but was unsure what the design was about. Researching the initials M.W.A., I found that it was a rosette for the Modern Woodmen of America.

Modern Woodmen of America (MWA) is one of the largest fraternal benefit societies in the United States, with more than

750,000 members. Its headquarters is currently located in Rock Island, Illinois. The society was founded by Joseph Cullen Root on January 5, 1883, in Lyons, Iowa. He had operated several businesses, including a mercantile establishment, a grain elevator and two flour mills. He sold insurance and real estate, taught bookkeeping classes, managed a lecture bureau, and practiced law. Root was a member of several fraternal societies throughout the years. He wanted to create an organization that would protect families following the death of a breadwinner. During a Sunday sermon, Root heard the pastor tell a parable about pioneer woodmen clearing away forests to build homes, communities and security for their families. He adopted the term "woodmen" for his organization. To complete the name, he added "modern" to reflect the need to stay current and change with the times, and "of America" to symbolize patriotism.

The Armistice Day rally was scheduled to begin at 2:00 PM. Russel was nervous for the parade to start. He was the youngest member of the local Modern Woodmen of America chapter in Sacred Heart, Minnesota. The Chapter President had asked Russel to lead the club on horseback in the parade. Although the parade was meant to honor the boys coming home from the war in France, Russel thought maybe it would be a chance to show off his horse skills and hopefully the town folk would be so impressed that they would forget that he didn't serve in the army.

Russel wanted to sign up with the rest of his buddies who joined the service in the spring of 1917, but was denied due to a birth defect that left one of his legs two inches shorter than the other. Many of the town folk understood Russel's medical condition, but a few thought he was just a coward for not going. To fight the social stigma and to help out the war effort, Russel began selling war bonds.

Russel's condition made walking difficult. While growing up he was constantly teased about it. When Russel turned eighteen, his father bought him a horse. From that day forward, Russel and his horse who he named Jack, were inseparable. Russel and Jack were always seen together. When riding Jack, Russel seemed to forget that he had a handicap. Many in town even seemed to forget as well. "Hello

Russel, how are you and Jack doing today?" people would ask from the sidewalk. "Doing great, trying to do my part for the war effort," Russel would yell back.

His involvement with the Woodmen began one spring afternoon, when Russel was in town selling bonds; he rode by the Catholic Church. A group of men were gathered on the front lawn. "What's going on?" Russel asked one of the men. "We are forming a men's club in town called the Woodmen," the assigned President said. After an awkward pause, Russel asked what it would take to join? "How old are you boy?" the man asked. "I'll be nineteen in November," Russel said. "Why aren't you off fighting the Kaiser?" another man piped in. "I would but I don't walk right," Russel said. "That's a well-mannered horse you have there boy," the man continued. Russel quickly responded, "His name is Jack, I named him after General Black Jack Pershing." "I like your patriotism," the President said.

As it turned out the new club was looking for a good horseman to lead parades. The best way to attract new members was to participate in all the surrounding town celebrations and events. "We need a club mascot and Jack is perfect," the President said.

All through the spring and summer of 1918, Russel and his horse Jack traveled with the Woodmen Society to all the local events. Russel

Bridle Rosettes

rode in the parades and when the parade was over, sold war bonds to anyone he could convince. The club bought Russel a new saddle and bridle to be used only for club events. On the saddle Russel had his name engraved in the leather and the new bridle was adorned with two beautiful glass dome rosettes.

Finally, the big day for the Sacred Heart parade had arrived. What would the local people say when they saw Russel following the Doughboys down main street. All the soldiers were decked out in their finely pressed uniforms. It was their day to be recognized and Russel felt uncomfortable even being a part of the event.

When the parade was over, Russel couldn't believe what happened. The entire group of soldiers and many town folk gathered around Russel and his horse Jack. "You have done more for the war cause than any of us," one soldier said. "I give a lot of credit to my partner Jack," Russel said with a smile. Russel knew that without Jack he would have never been able to raise all the money he did.

Later that evening, when Russel got home and was putting Jack in the barn, he noticed that one of the rosettes was missing from the bridle. I'll go back to town tomorrow and look for it on the street, it must have fallen off somewhere on the parade route, he thought. _U_

 1918

March 4 » A soldier at Camp Funston, Kansas falls sick with the first confirmed case of the Spanish flu.

March 19 » The U.S. Congress establishes time zones and approves daylight saving time.

October 12 » 1918 Cloquet Fire: The city of Cloquet, Minnesota and nearby areas are destroyed in a fire, killing 453.

November 11 » World War I ends.

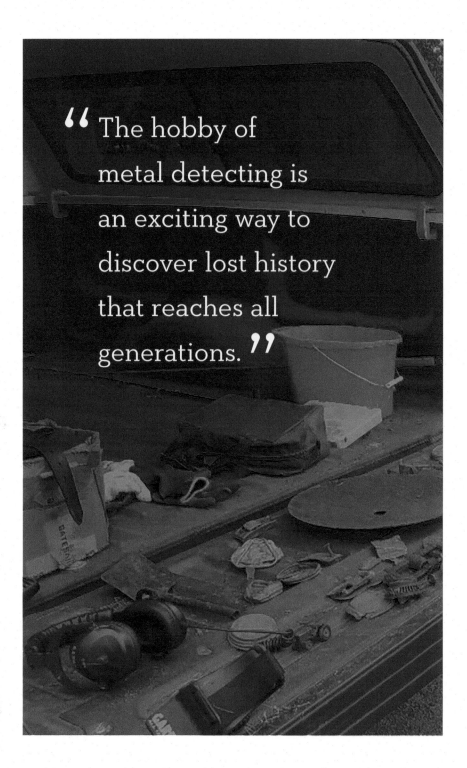

" The hobby of
metal detecting is
an exciting way to
discover lost history
that reaches all
generations. "

Tootsie Toys

CHAPTER 3

Toys

Years ago kids left a lot of toys outside and in time they sank into the ground and were seemingly lost forever — until years later I come along with my metal detector and bring them back to life. It seems like a lot of boys and girls lost their toy cars or cap guns. Over the years I have found well over one hundred Tootsie, Matchbox and Hot Wheels. I enjoy recovering the depression era toys the most. It is not hard to imagine how important that toy was to a child who may not have had much. Holding it in my hand and just knowing that the last time this toy was held, eighty or ninety years ago, is very meaningful for me.

Toy Guns

The Big Race

Imagine my surprise to discover what might be the coolest toy I have ever found while metal detecting. After a rainy morning in SE Minnesota, I stopped at a historic church in the small town of Oronoco to do some afternoon hunting. This toy was manufactured by the Tootsie Toy Company in 1937 and was called the Buck Rogers Rocket Ship Battlecruiser. It was withdrawn from production after only one year due to limited sales. This toy operated on a string that ran through a set of wheel pulleys. The other end of the string was tied to a stationary object such as a wall. By moving the string the spaceship would slide back and forth on the string giving the feeling of flight.

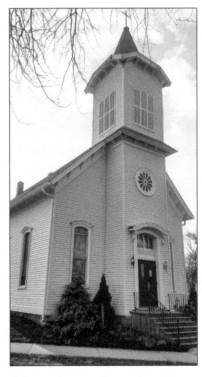

Tootsie Toys! There is magic in the name for those who remember playing with them in childhood. To an entire generation of children these toys are sure to bring back the days when a nickel or a dime bought hours of fun and imagination. Most Tootsie Toys were simple in construction made of metal as a miniature replica of a real vehicle. The company made toys starting in 1910 and lasting into the early 1960s. The majority of Tootsie Toys were cars and trucks. Today there is a strong collection community that treasures these toys.

Tommy couldn't wait for his birthday to come. He was counting the days and before long June 21st arrived. Tommy had always bragged to his friends that his birthday lasted the longest because it landed on the longest day of the year. Grandma and Grandpa were coming over that morning to celebrate. Although times were tough, Tommy knew that on this day at least, his grandparents would spoil him.

When they arrived, Grandpa held the small brown wrapped package that Tommy knew was a birthday present. After lunch and the dishes cleaned up, mom had Tommy sit at the head of the dining room table in dad's seat. She brought out a colorful cone shaped birthday hat along with Tommy's favorite chocolate fudge cake with 10 candles. Tommy's dad lit them and soon the room was filled with the singing of "Happy Birthday." Normally Tommy took his time eating his mother's cake, savoring every bite, but today he stuffed the cake down and claimed he was ready for gifts. "Don't be impolite," his mother chided. Everyone else just laughed as they were just excited to move the party forward.

At first Tommy did not know what the toy was or how it worked. It came with a small folded instruction sheet and soon Tommy had the string attached to stairway railing and was flying his new Buck Rogers battlecruiser.

The next day was Sunday and as always Tommy and his folks along with Grandma and Grandpa went to the local Presbyterian Church. This Sunday service was the same as many others, but that afternoon it was the annual Sunday school picnic. The picnic would start with a lunch followed by games for the kids, a softball game for the men and finally the day would end with fireworks over Lake Oronoco.

Tommy was excited to show his Sunday school friends his birthday present. Mom told him to be careful not to lose it in all the day's excitement. The boys were especially in awe of the battlecruiser, the girls not so much.

It wasn't long before Mr. Olson called the boys and girls together to pair them for the traditional three-legged race. Tommy was happy he was paired up with Ben, who was tall for his age and the best of all the boys in sports. Stuffing the battlecruiser into his top bib overall pocket, Tommy waited with Ben for the race gun to go off. They would have won, but Tommy couldn't keep up with Ben's long stride and after three falls, they came in third.

In all the days excitement, Tommy forgot about his birthday present. The next day he realized it was not in the pocket he remembered putting it in. Tommy's dad said that they would look for it the next Sunday, but the gift was never found. The following Monday, Grandpa took Tommy to Rochester to buy a replacement. Tommy treasured the new toy for years. Today he keeps it in a special glass bookcase to remind him of his grandfather and that special tenth birthday.

TIMELINE ⟩ 1937

January 11 » The first issue of Look magazine goes on sale.

May 6 » Hindenburg disaster: The German airship Hindenburg bursts into flame when mooring to a mast in Lakehurst, New Jersey.

June 2 » Amelia Earhart and navigator Fred Noonan disappear after taking off from New Guinea during Earhart's attempt to become the first woman to fly around the world.

December 21 » Walt Disney's Snow White and the Seven Dwarfs, the first feature-length animated cartoon with sound, opens and becomes a smash hit.

The Promise

FACTS I was out at an old farm site near Clearwater, Minnesota, and was about to quit for the day since all I was finding were Mason jar lids, scraps of old cans and of course a lot of nails. While walking back to my truck, I got a good signal and to my surprise, I dug up this old toy car. I knew it was old because of the weight. Most new toys have a lot of plastic and are much lighter. The style of the car was also a clue to its possible age. When I got home, I cleaned it up and began the research. I have a couple of good reference books on old toys and before long, I found my treasure listed. It was made by the Tootsie Toy Company in the 1930s and was considered desirable and cost more than most of their toys.

Bernard was happy to just have a job. He had been laid off from the county last month and was lucky to have found a night job at the small cheese factory within walking distance from home. Bernard and his wife Lois were married less than a year and were renting an old run down farm place. The place wasn't much to look at, but the rent was only twenty-five dollars a month. With Lois now pregnant and unable to work, Bernard took as many hours as the factory would give him.

The Limburger Cheese Factory, as it was locally known, had been in business in the small village of Hasty since the turn of the last century. Bernard's job was general maintenance and cleaning the wooden vats, but occasionally when they were down a man, he worked in delivery. After his first week on the job, he couldn't even smell the strong cheese odor that at first almost took his breath away. Lois never got used to the smell and made him take his work clothes off in the barn before coming into the house. Her pregnancy and the off-putting odor of Limburger made her wonder if she should go to her folks in Foley until after the baby was born. She didn't go, but thought about it almost every day that summer of 1936.

By mid-September, baby Matthew arrived after a mad dash to the hospital in St. Cloud in the borrowed cheese delivery truck. Bernard drove well over the speed limit as Lois clutched a cheese crate begging him to hurry. The baby was born healthy and both Lois and Bernard knew their lives would never be the same.

As little Matthew grew into a toddler, he would beg his dad to take him along in the delivery truck. He never tired of watching his dad drive, but his favorite part of the drive, was all of the stops. Every store they delivered to had a toy aisle and occasionally his dad let him have a few minutes to look around. On one particular delivery to Monticello, Matthew spotted a toy he had never seen before. It was a car that looked like cars only rich people drove. Matthew begged his dad for the car, but was told it was too expensive. "I'll do extra chores for it," Matthew pleaded. Dad broke down and bought the toy, but told Matthew that he would have to keep it a secret from mom. "She would never understand," he said "it's not your birthday or Christmas." "I'll keep it in the back yard and only play with it outside," Matthew promised.

HISTORICAL NOTE » Tootsie cars and trucks were made with only seven parts. Four wheels, two axels on a cast body. Tootsietoy is a manufacturer of die cast toy cars and other toy vehicles which was based in Chicago, Illinois. The Tootsietoy name has been used since before the 1920s. The companies' origins date from about 1890. An enduring marque, toys with the Tootsietoy name were consistently popular from the 1930s through the 1960s.

⫸ TIMELINE ⫸ 1936

March 1 » Construction of Hoover Dam is completed.

June 10 » Margaret Mitchell's epic historical romance Gone with the Wind is published.

August 3 » African-American athlete Jesse Owens wins the 100-meter dash at the Berlin Olympics.

November 3 » U.S. presidential election, 1936: Democrat Franklin D. Roosevelt is reelected to a second term in a landslide victory over Republican Governor of Kansas Alf Landon.

1970's Tootsie Baby Blue Porsche

Early Birthday Present

FACTS I got to know eighty-four-year-old Elden Tessman a few years ago when I stopped by his farm in Brooklyn Park to ask if he would help me with a barn bus tour I was putting together. Elden and I soon became good friends, mainly because we both love history. His place is one of the oldest intact farmsteads in Hennepin County. It dates to the 1860s and the old barn is still standing.

I asked Elden if he would mind if I scanned the yard around the old house with my metal detector. After about an hour of finding old farm relics, I got a signal that rang up as a coin. Digging down about four inches, I found this small pin badge. I immediately asked Elden about it, thinking he might know what it was, but he claimed he had no idea. I took it home and began the research.

The Howie Wing badge was distributed by Kellogg's. Howie Wing was a children's radio show written by a World War I flying reservist, who foiled spies and smugglers with some fancy flying, which debuted in 1938. The success of the show was propagated by the multitude of gimmicks and prizes that grew up around the show, one of which was the cadet wing that was available to anyone with a few Kellogg's Cornflakes box tops. Kellogg's was looking for a wholesome children's show and Howie Wing apparently, was just the thing.

Boys! Girls! Here's your chance to join a real national aviation club!...wear the official Corps Wings of glistening chromium that only members can have! You'll be in an outfit with thousands of other wide-awake, air-minded American boys and girls. And in an outfit with real flyers! Yes, many of the nation's leading airmen belong to the Cadet Aviation Corps as Senior Pilots, so you can see that the club is the real thing! (Script date, January 6, 1939)

Even at the age of ten, Dianne knew that living on a farm in Brooklyn Park was not that exciting. Her parents Harris and Wilma had moved their small family around a lot during the past few years looking for work. The economic depression had affected many families.

Harris had known George Tessman since high school. They had played football together in Osseo. Harris heard that his old friend was looking for a foreman on his rapidly expanding potato farm. Harris had worked on several farms the past few years, mainly on threshing crews, but he needed the steady work and this opportunity sounded good.

As foreman, Harris was given the small farm house to live in that was directly across the road from the Tessmans. Harris and Wilma were relieved that they could finally settle down and provide their only daughter, Dianne, a house larger than a one-bedroom apartment. At first Dianne was excited with the new place. She spent the first few days on the farm exploring the out buildings and riding her bike up and down the dirt road. She was hoping to find other kids her age to play with nearby.

The summer of 1938 was moving at a boring pace for Dianne. No girls her age lived close. The nearest neighbor kid was Allen Tessman, who was two years younger than her. Most days Dianne and Allen would either ride bikes together or play in the hay mow of the barn making forts and swinging on the rope that hung down from the hay track. One day in late July, Allen appeared in the yard wearing a shiny small winged badge on his shirt. Dianne asked about it and Allen replied "it came in yesterday's mail." He told Dianne that he sent in three Cornflakes cereal box tops and now he was part of the Howie Wing Club. "I want to be a part of the club too," Dianne said. "You can't," snapped Allen, "it's for boys only and besides you need to ask your mom to send in three cereal box tops and I know you can't do that because you folks are poor."

Dianne rushed home upset with Allen and told her mom that she wanted to be a Howie Cadet. "A what?" her mom asked. Dianne told her the story about Allen and his winged badge. Her mom said that she was sorry that Allen had been so mean, but told her that later that day she would forget all about the cadet badge. Dianne was puzzled.

Just before supper that day, the local postman knocked at the door with a large box with Dianne's name on it. To her surprise, inside the

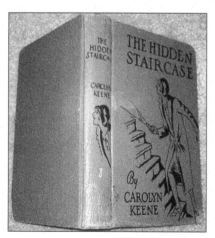

box she found a three-book set of Nancy Drew Mysteries. "It's an early Birthday present," her mom said. Dianne couldn't believe it; she now had the first three books in the series which included her favorite "The Hidden Staircase." She had read a borrowed copy from the library, but never thought she would be able start her own collection.

The very next day, she went over to Allen's house with the first book "The Secret of the Old Clock." They sat under one of the large maple trees in the front yard and Dianne began reading aloud.

Before the summer was over, Dianne and Allen had made their way through all three mysteries. What began as a boring summer, turned out to be a summer Dianne would never forget as she got lost in the excitement of solving mysteries with Nancy Drew. Allen seemed to lose interest in the Howie Cadet club as he himself couldn't wait for the next chapter in Dianne's book.

 1938

January 3 » The March of Dimes is established as a foundation to combat infant polio by President Franklin D. Roosevelt.

July 3 » The last reunion of the Blue and Gray commemorates the 75th anniversary of the Battle of Gettysburg in Gettysburg, Pennsylvania.

October 24 » The minimum wage is established by law in the U.S.

November 10 » On the eve of Armistice Day, Kate Smith sings Irving Berlin's "God Bless America" for the first time on her weekly radio show.

Toy Gun

The Burn

1st hunt

FACTS At first, I didn't know what I had found. I was hunting in the woods near a lake in central Minnesota when I got a loud consistent signal on the detector. Digging down about 5 inches, I pulled out what looked like a chunk of iron. After closer inspection, I saw that it had a design on it. Later when I got home and cleaned it with water, the design became clear. I had found one half of a toy soldier mold. About a month later I went back to the same

2nd Hunt

woods to see if I could find the matching piece. No luck with that, but I did find another mold with a different design. How old were these and how did they ever get in the middle of the woods? I thought.

The Lead Soldier Casting Set was made by the Rapco Company. They originally came with two pairs of mold halves, the mold clamps and handles, the electric stove and ladle, as well as 30 pigs (ingots) of casting lead. The toy dates to the late 1950s through the 1960s. In the early 1970s the toy was taken off the market due to dangers to children.

Rapco Castright Metal Casting Sets, cited by the National Commission on Product Safety as producing 800 degrees of heat inside the stove and 500 to 600 degrees on its surfaces. This according to a New York Times article from 1971.

"Ouch that hurt," Ricky said as he picked up the lead soldier the from the kitchen table. Ricky's older brother Rusty had just taken a completed lead soldier out of the mold to cool. "It's your own fault. I told you to wait. Besides, you will wreck them if they're not ready," Rusty said in an agitate tone. "I'm telling mom and dad that you made some soldiers when they weren't home," Ricky said in retaliation. Rusty knew that mom and dad had made strict rules about when he could play with his casting set. "Ok Ok," Rusty said, "you can play with them, just don't squeal on me and be careful."

Rusty had just turned eleven and all he asked for his birthday was a lead soldier casting set. His best friend Barry got one for Christmas and Rusty just had to have one himself. "No way are you getting one of those," his mother said. "They're dangerous and you would probably burn the house down." Begging had worked before and Rusty thought he would try it again along with talking with his dad. Maybe, just maybe, dad would think the casting set was cool and convince mom that he was old enough to be responsible.

It worked and Rusty got his soldier mold casting set. "You have to agree to the rules," his dad said. "Oh, I will," Rusty replied. "No playing with the set without your mother or me being home. Is that clear?" his dad stressed. "Crystal," Rusty said with a smirk. "Don't get smart with me boy," his dad yelled back. "I still have the Montgomery Ward's receipt and can return it just like that," his dad snapped his fingers.

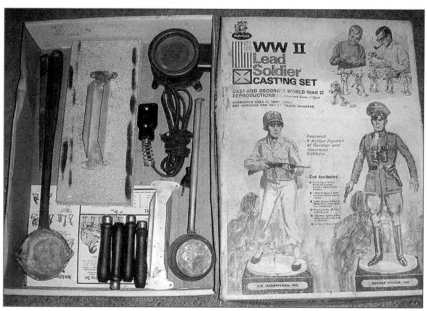

Metal Casting Set

"You wouldn't really do that would you?" Rusty asked. "Just watch me," his dad said as he left the room.

"I won't squeal," Ricky said, "But I get to pour the next batch of hot lead." "Just be careful," Rusty warned again. "If you burn yourself mom and dad will know we played with it when they weren't home." With a defying look Ricky said, "Do you think I'm a baby?" "Sometimes, I know you're a baby," Rusty said laughing.

As Ricky was pouring the lead into the last hole in the mold, he slipped and hot lead spilled out all over his left hand. Screaming in pain Ricky ran to the sink and turned on the cold water. Rusty sat in shock as if the whole thing happened in slow motion. Looking at Ricky's hand, Rusty knew he had to do something. I'll call next door to the Johnson's and see if Mavis can help, Rusty thought. Picking up the phone, Rusty could barely hear the party line conversation over the screams of Ricky at the sink. "I need help," Rusty interrupted into the phone. Like usual, Mavis was on the phone gossiping to one of the church ladies. Rusty almost in tears, quickly explained what happened. "Stop crying, I'll be right over;" Mavis said as she hung up the phone, "I know just what to do."

"What am I going to tell mom and dad?" Rusty said as Mavis applied some burn cream to Ricky's hand. "It's only a minor burn," Mavis said, "but always remember honesty is best."

That was the last of the soldier casting set either Rusty or Ricky ever saw. Dad took it away, but would never tell the boys what he did with it. 🚗

TIMELINE ▷ 1966

February 9 » The National Hockey League awarded the Twin Cities area an NHL franchise, the Minnesota North Stars.

March 26 » Demonstrations are held across the United States against the Vietnam War.

April 18 » The 38th Academy Awards ceremony is held; The Sound of Music wins Best Picture.

August 29 » The Beatles play their very last concert at Candlestick Park in San Francisco, California.

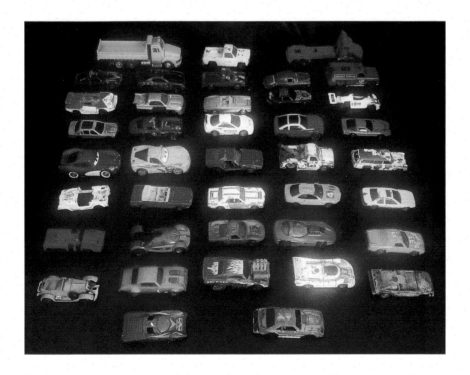

You're Now Official

FACTS I was detecting at a local park near an elementary school when I got a good signal a few inches down. At first, I thought it was a real fireman's badge, but soon realized it was a toy. The badge was in great condition with only the pin on the back missing. I took it home and cleaned it up and began the research.

In the late 1950s, Tonka Toy Company included a Chief badge in the Tonka Fire Department set. The set not only included the badge, but three vehicles including an Aerial Ladder Truck, Pumper Truck and an Emergency Rescue vehicle.

The present under the Christmas tree was the biggest gift Joey had ever seen. The big box was wrapped in red checkered paper with a large white bow and a tag that said "To: Joey, From: Mom and Dad."

"When do we get to open gifts?" Joey pleaded to his Mom. "Next Sunday is Christmas Eve and if your dad isn't too exhausted from working double shifts at the station, we can do gifts after church" his mother said.

All week-long Joey could hardly keep from ripping into the big red package. "Joey, if I told you once I've told you a million times. Do not touch the gifts under the tree," his mother said. "I know," Joey admitted, "It's just hard being a kid."

Wednesday of that week, Joey found himself home alone. Dad was at the Hopkins fire station and mom was scheduled to help the church youth leaders on final preparations for the Christmas play. Joey had turned ten years old that November and had convinced his mom that

a baby sitter was not needed. "Just listen to the Sugar Creek Gang on the radio and I'll be home before you know it," his mother said. Every Wednesday night Joey loved following the boys in the gang, especially, Big Jim and Dragonfly. "Don't worry Mom, I'll be just fine," Joey said.

After the Sugar Creek Gang program was over Joey noticed that it was dark outside so he plugged in the Christmas tree lights. It was then that he saw the big red box again under the tree. "Maybe he could carefully un-wrap just a small corner and see what it was," he thought. He remembered where Mom kept the Scotch tape and could use it if he had to. Carefully Joey began to un-wrap the gift. Before long,

due to his excitement, he had made a mess of things. "I'm in big trouble" he kept repeating to himself as he pulled more wrapping paper away. Soon most of the paper was off the box. In big bold red letters he saw the word "TONKA".

"What is a Tonka?" Joey said out loud to himself. Still confused, Joey began to try to wrap up the box again with the torn red paper. Using a lot of Mom's tape, he thought he did a pretty good job. If he covered the box with other gifts and pushed it further under the tree, maybe, just maybe his secret wouldn't be noticed.

For the rest of the week, Joey hardly even looked at the Christmas tree. His eyes might give it away, he thought. Sunday soon arrived and after church, Dad suggested that they open gifts. Mom noticed that Joey didn't seem that excited. "What's wrong Joey?" she asked. Joey wanted to come clean, but was so scared that he said he had a tummy ache. "I'll be ok," Joey lied. Dad began handing out gifts and soon picked up the big red box. "Who wrapped this one? He said with a laugh. It looks like one of Santa's elves needs more training." Joey quickly looked over to his Mom and was relieved when she responded with "Oh Ken, just give the boy his gift." Joey quickly tore into the wrapping paper before anyone would notice and soon forgot all about what he had done a few days before.

Joey loved the Tonka Fireman's set, but mostly loved that it came with an official badge. "You're now official," his dad said as he pinned it on Joey's shirt. "I'm just like you dad," Joey said with a grin.

Later that night as Mom was tucking Joey into bed, she said "I know what you did on Wednesday night." "Am I in trouble?" Joey asked. "No Joey," she said sweetly, I was a kid once a long time ago and understand the excitement of Christmas."

When school started again in January, Joey made sure that he wore his fire chief badge on his winter coat every day. One day after an aggressive game of King of the Hill at recess, Joey noticed his badge was gone. He and a couple of friends searched for it near the hill after school, but were never able to find it.

HISTORICAL NOTE » Tonka is an American producer of toy trucks. Mound Metalcraft was created in 1946 in Mound, Minnesota, by Lynn Everett Baker, Avery F. Crounse, and Alvin F. Tesch. Their original intent was to manufacture garden implements. Their building's former occupant, the Streater Company, had made and patented several toys. E. C. Streater was not interested in the toy business so they approached Mound Metalcraft. The three men at Mound Metalcraft thought they might make a good side line to their other products.

After some modifications to the design by Alvin Tesch and the addition of a new logo created by Erling Eklof, the company began selling metal toys, which soon became the primary business. The logo was based on a University of Minnesota drafting student's sketch by Donald B. Olson, who later became the company's chief industrial engineer. The logo used the Dakota Sioux word Tanka, which means "great" or "big". In November, 1955, Mound Metalcraft changed its name to Tonka Toys Incorporated. The logo at this time was an oval, showing the Tonka Toys name in red above waves, presumably honoring nearby Lake Minnetonka.

 1960

January 2 » U.S. Senator John F. Kennedy (D-MA) announces his candidacy for the Democratic presidential nomination.

May 1 » A Soviet missile shoots down an American Lockheed U-2 spy plane; the pilot Gary Powers is captured.

June 16 » The film Psycho is released, directed by Alfred Hitchcock.

December 9 » The first Domino's Pizza location opens in Ypsilanti, Michigan.

Toy Train Car

" Metal detecting is the closest you will get to time travel. We unearth the scattered memories, find the stories and fill in the personality. "

— *Detectorists*

Scouts Neckerchief Slide

Lipstick Tube

Silver Ring

CHAPTER 4

Personal Relics

I t seems that most days I go metal detecting I find treasures of a personal nature. Sometimes it is an old belt buckle, makeup compact, or a vintage lip stick tube. I have found many custom jewelry items such as rings and earrings, but on occasion I do find the real thing. A silver ring or gold earring can make your day metal detecting.

Silver Cross

Suspenders Buckle

The Blizzard of 1888

FACTS In 2015, my friend Jay Grammond and I ventured off for a metal detecting weekend in central North Dakota. We were both pretty inexperienced metal detectorists, but what we lacked in knowledge, we made up for in enthusiasm. We had received permission to hunt on a farm that backed up to Sibley Lake. The lake was named for General Henry Sibley who in the summer 1863 camped with a large number of soldiers during the Indian wars of the Dakotas.

We didn't find any military relics on this trip, but we did find these two pieces of local history. Both the women's pocket knife and the old ice skate were found on the shore of the lake only a few yards from each other. The knife is from 1880s and we believe that the ice skate is in that time frame as well. How did they get there and are their stories connected?

The weather looked like snow was on the way when Violet arrived at Mary's farm with the promised picnic basket lunch. The two girls were neighbors and were excited to get one more ice-skating outing in before the snows of midwinter would cover the lake ice. Early January could be great skating on shallow Sibley Lake and the girls knew they would have the entire lake to themselves.

As they hiked over the hill that separated the farm from the lake, they were hit by a strong gust of wind that made them both look at each other and wonder the same thing. Would the day be cut short due to the weather? They knew they wouldn't have all day to skate as they had hoped. Finding a hillside cliff to keep out of the wind, the girls quickly strapped on their metal clamp skates. Both girls were very good skaters and would often race from one side of the lake to the other. Violet usually won, but it was all in good sport. They skated along the shoreline at first, daring each other to go further out, but quickly coming back toward shore when they would hear a large ice boom. Laughing and calling each other chicken, the girls finally took a break and broke out their packed lunches. Mary was excited to show Violet her new pocket knife she had purchased a few weeks ago when she traveled to Fargo with her folks. The knife had a corkscrew and two blades. It was perfect for cutting the two apples from their lunch.

After lunch the skating resumed and before long the afternoon sun began to set and the wind started to pick up. The snow seemed to come out of nowhere. Within minutes the sky turned a dark grey and the girls could hardly find the spot where they had left their boots and half eaten lunch. In the haste to get their skates off and boots laced for the hike back over the hill, Violet accidently dropped a skate and Mary didn't see the pocket knife that laid half buried in the fresh snow.

The girls did make it back to the Mary's farm, but just in time. The storm would always be remembered as the Schoolhouse Blizzard of 1888. 🔷

HISTORICAL NOTE » The blizzard hit the U.S. plains states on January 12, 1888. It came unexpectedly on a relatively warm day, and many people were caught unaware, including children in one-room schoolhouses. The blizzard was precipitated by the collision of an immense Arctic cold front with warm moisture-laden air from the Gulf of Mexico. Within a few hours, the advancing cold front caused a temperature drop from a few degrees above freezing to -20 degrees Fahrenheit in some places. This wave of cold was accompanied by high winds and heavy snow. The fast-moving storm first struck Montana in the early hours of January 12, swept through Dakota Territory from midmorning to early afternoon, and reached Lincoln, Nebraska at 3 p.m.

 1888

January 13 » The National Geographic Society is founded in Washington, D.C.

August 5 » Bertha Benz arrives in Pforzheim having driven 40 miles (64 km) from Mannheim in a car manufactured by her husband Karl Benz, thus completing the first "long-distance" drive in the history of the automobile.

September 4 » In the United States, George Eastman registers the trademark Kodak, and receives a patent for his camera, which uses roll film.

October 9 » The Washington Monument officially opens to the general public, in Washington, D.C.

Gold
Tie Bar

Snowball Fight

I called Pastor Steve Johnston to gain permission to metal detect in the yard of the Snake River Church near Big Lake, MN. I knew the church was old and thought it may have never been detected. Starting on the north side of the church I found a couple old coins and my share of roofing nails. I moved to the south side of the building later that day and to my surprise I found this white gold earring. At first, I thought it was a piece

of cheap costume jewelry, but after cleaning it I found the maker's mark. It dates to the 1940s and was made by the Monet Company.

The company was established by brothers Michael and Jay Chernow and was initially known as the Monocraft Products Company, which manufactured gold- and silver- plated monogram plaques for use in women's handbags. Monocraft bags were highly sought-after and well-known for their quality.

However, it was only in the late 1930s that Monocraft began to focus on jewelry. Because of the economic crisis of the late 1920s, many women couldn't afford fine jewelry and costume jewelry became an excellent alternative. The company saw this as an opportunity to capitalize on. 1937, the company's name was changed to Monet and began producing high-quality costume jewelry. Led by Edmond Granville, a former Cartier fine jewelry designer, the company transformed into a leading fashion brand. Since then, Monet Jewelry has changed hands many times, and was purchased in 2000 by Liz Claiborne. Today the brand remains a favorite for vintage costume jewelry collectors and is still sought-after by those who love vintage designs.

The church basement was as festive with red and green decorations as anyone had ever remembered seeing it. Some of the young people had spent all afternoon running colorful streamers from wall to wall, putting out little paper Santa Clauses with reindeer on the tables, getting things just right. Tonight, was the big event for all the youth. Kids from as far away as Elk River and St. Cloud were expected to join the kids from the Snake River church. Of course, the weather would determine if many of them would make the drive. The church had promoted the youth event in the local newspapers as a nondenominational safe party for kids.

JoAnne was hoping that her mom would let her wear makeup and put on lipstick for the evening. Her favorite holiday had always been Christmas and tonight was a special night. Her father had returned from the fighting near the 38th Parallel in Korea the week before. He was going to dress up like Santa and surprise all the kids at the party.

Just before JoAnne left for the party, her mom surprised her by giving the Ok for the makeup and even sweetened the night by letting JoAnne wear her gold clip-on earrings. This night was starting better than JoAnne could have ever dreamed. She would ride with her best friend Julie. Julie's dad would drive the girls so not to give away the Santa surprise.

The party was going perfect for everyone until a few of the annoying boys noticed it had started to snow and suggested a boys against girls snowball fight outside. The kids all rushed to get their coats, hats and gloves on to begin the battle. JoAnne forgot about the earrings she had on as the snowballs began to be thrown. One older boy named Ned threw an extra-large snowball at JoAnne that hit her in the head. Although it didn't hurt much, JoAnne got revenge and stuffed snow down Ned's back. The snowball fight was soon over and everyone went back inside for some hot chocolate. Just then, JoAnne realized one of her Moms earrings was missing. In a panic, she asked everyone to get dressed again and help her look for it outside. Of course, everyone helped, but no amount of searching was enough to ever find the lost earring.

TIMELINE 1951

January 10 » The new United Nations headquarters officially opens in New York City.

March 6 » Second Red Scare: Ethel and Julius Rosenberg stand trial facing charges of conspiracy to commit espionage.

April 11 » U.S. President Harry S. Truman relieves General Douglas MacArthur of his Far Eastern commands.

November 10 » Direct dial coast-to-coast telephone service begins.

Summer Job

As metal detectorists most of us began our hobby by going to places that we were familiar with. That was the case with the location I found this vintage pocket watch.

Growing up near St. Francis, Minnesota, we had favorite lakes for swimming and fishing. My favorite swimming lake was Norris Lake. It had a small beach, but great sand and few rocks and the lake water was incredibly clear. The beach area closed in the mid-1970s and has become overgrown and would be unrecognizable as a former beach to most people. I thought this spot could have great potential for finding lost history. I wasn't disappointed. This pocket watch is just one of many historic treasures I have found along this lake shore.

Robert H. Ingersoll and his brother Charles founded the Ingersoll Watch Company, one of the oldest American watchmakers. The Ingersoll brothers were pioneers of industry and invention in the field of watchmaking. They devised and followed an ambitious plan: to offer Ingersoll watches to the general public at an affordable price, whilst maintaining real quality and credibility.

Norris Lake

Based in New York City, each watch was initially produced by hand, but in 1892, thanks to Henry Ford, Ingersoll succeeded in developing a production line for pocket watches and wristwatches.

With high quality production, precision components and the very reasonable price of $1.00 (a day's wages at that time) the so-called 'Dollar Watch' was born.

The Dollar Watch was so popular that over one million were sold. Ingersoll watches have been sold continuously since their inception and today the Ingersoll brand is renowned the world over.

It was hard for Willie, being the youngest in the family, especially that summer in 1923 when most of his brothers were leaving for Boy Scout camp that last week in June. He was too young to go with them and knew it would be the longest two weeks of his life. At six years of age, he wondered what he was supposed to do for fun.

His oldest brother Danny didn't go to camp that summer because he had a job at a nearby truck farm weeding radishes. Danny had bragged about how much money he was going to make while the other guys were gone to camp. Willie remembered years later, that Monday afternoon when Danny came home early from the radish farm. "I quit," Danny said. "They drive us like dogs and I can't work for people like that."

The next day started what would be the best summer of Willie's young life. He and Danny were about to become rich. Their farmer neighbor, Paul Moore, suggested that the boys start trapping gophers. "You know boys, the county is paying 10 cents per gopher and if you want, you can start trapping in my pasture." With some loaner traps and a little instruction from Mr. Moore, Danny and little Willie created their own trap line.

At first, they came up empty, but before long they got the hang of things and their luck changed. Danny would set the trap by standing on the lever being very careful not to release his foot before the pin was set correctly. Because Willie's hands were so small, he gently slid the open trap into the gopher tunnel then covered it with dirt. The next morning the boys would check the traps and if they got one, Danny would grab the long trap chain and Willie would stand ready with the baseball bat for the final kill. Their system worked and by the end of the two weeks they had 36 pocket gophers to their credit.

That Friday before the other brothers returned from scout camp, Danny and Willie brought their gophers to the Anoka County courthouse to get their bounty. Each received $1.80 in cash. After getting his money, Willie was unsure what he wanted to buy. The boys walked down see their grandmother who worked at the Jackson Hotel. They wanted to show her their windfall. It was in the side lobby of the hotel that Willie saw the bearded man selling pocket watches. "Only a dollar," the man yelled. That was enough for Willie. He bought the first one he saw.

On Saturday after Willies brothers came home, Dad and Mom took the whole family on a special outing to Norris Lake for a picnic and a day of swimming. Willie of course brought his new pocket watch just to annoy everyone by announcing the time every ten minutes. While Willie was swimming, two of his brothers hid the watch in the tall grass and due to the day's excitement, Willie forgot to make sure he had it when they returned home. Sadly, Willie never found his watch and it wasn't until years later that his brothers admitted to the crime. 🔆

March 2 ⟫ The first issue of Time magazine is published.

April 18 ⟫ The first Yankee Stadium opens its doors in the Bronx, New York City.

July 13 ⟫ The Hollywood Sign is inaugurated in California.

August 2 ⟫ Vice President Calvin Coolidge becomes the 30th President of the United States, upon the death of President Warren G. Harding.

Cameo Ring

Small Gift

FACTS As a photographer and public speaker I often get the opportunity to travel extensively throughout Minnesota. Frequently I have free time between events which allows me to do some photography and metal detecting. A few years ago, I was on a speaking tour in northern Minnesota and had an afternoon free. An old house near the highway caught my eye. It didn't look like anyone was living there and there wasn't a "No Trespassing" sign posted. I drove to the nearest farm to inquire about the property. I was told that the house wasn't occupied and the owner ran a resort campground nearby. I drove to the campground and met the owner and his wife. I asked them if I could scan my detector in the yard of the old house and they immediately gave me the OK. They have owned the house for a number of years and had plans to clean it up and do some remodeling. Their long-term goals for the property were uncertain. They said the house dates to the late 1800s. I thanked them and told them I would report back if I found a cache of gold bullion. We all laughed at the thought of lost treasure just waiting to be found.

I didn't find any gold, but I did find a lot of old farming relics, a harmonica reed and my favorite find of the day, this small pocket knife.

Agnes waited all summer for a letter from Knute. He had gone to America the year before and promised Agnes that when he got settled, he would send for her. Before he left, she tried to convince him that they should marry in Norway and go to America together, but Knute had other ideas. He had read about wild beasts, savage Indians and other dangers in America and thought it best to go on ahead first.

Finally, the letter from Knute arrived and enclosed in the envelope was a one-way ticket on the White Star Line. Agnes couldn't pack fast enough. She had already said most of her goodbyes and if she had her way, would have skipped out on the going to America farewell party put on by all her aunts and girl cousins. The day after the party her mother and father took Agnes to the docks in Stavanger. The ship looked magical to Agnes. "It looks like a large wedding cake," she told her mother. "It will take me to my husband in America," she said with a smile. "You're not married yet," her dad said lightheartedly. "I won't be in America very long before we tie the knot. That I promise you," Agnes said as she hugged her mother and father for the last time. She knew that this goodbye would be their last.

Years later Agnes would tell her children about the long north Atlantic voyage coming to America. "At times the ocean waves would be as high as our house," she would say. The children would scream with excitement as she exaggerated the details. They truly loved her travel stories, but always asked her to repeat the story of her wedding day. That story was always their favorite even though they knew it by heart.

When Agnes stepped off the train in the small whistle stop town of McIntosh, Minnesota, she thought she had arrived at the end of the world. Knute was late arriving to pick her up due to a washed-out road from a recent storm. When he finally arrived, he found Agnes in tears. He tried to explain, but immediately Agnes didn't care, she was just happy to see her man. On the five-mile trip back to the farm on Oak Lake, they talked without stopping. "When can we get married?" Agnes kept asking. Knute repeated the same thing over and over, "as soon as the threshing is done." Agnes didn't understand the delay. Back in Norway harvest took only a day or two. "Why does it take so long?" she asked a little bit annoyed. Knute responded, "Our farm is one hundred and sixty acres. We also have to wait until the threshing crew can get to our place. It won't be our turn until later next week." Agnes realized there was so much she had to learn about her new country.

When she saw the beautiful white house for the first time with its black shutters, she started to cry. "All for me," she sobbed. "All for you, Knute said with a grin. I also have a small gift waiting for you in the house." Agnes opened the small box and found a personal yellow pocket knife. "It says Agnes Uggen on it, she said. That's not my name, we're not married Knute." "I know, but we will soon," he said with a sweet smile.

Knute and Agnes married that fall with a wedding on the shores of their lake and in time would have seven children. They farmed wheat until 1910, when they converted the farm to dairy. When Agnes passed away in 1936, the kids looked everywhere in the house for the keepsake pocket knife. They never knew their mother to be without it. Sadly, their search came up empty.

HISTORICAL NOTE » The dairy farm came to an end when the 4-lane highway went through the farm in 1969. The Oak Lake Rest Area and the Weigh Station were also built on the original Uggen farm.

Mother of Pearl
Cufflink

January 1 » Ellis Island begins receiving immigrants to the United States.

January 20 » At the YMCA in Springfield, Massachusetts, the first official basketball game is played.

February 12 » Former President Abraham Lincoln's birthday is declared a national public holiday in the United States.

May 28 » The Sierra Club is organized by John Muir in San Francisco, California.

Harmonica Reed

Shoe Buckle

Riverbank Proposal

I never ever thought I would find an actual gold engagement diamond ring metal detecting.

I was in a small city park in Northeast Minneapolis and was about to call it a day when I got a strange signal on the detector. Because I rarely find gold, I thought the signal was trash.

Curiosity won out and I'm glad it did. This white gold ring with a small diamond was about 4 inches deep. I knew it was real because of the weight. Costume jewelry tends to be much lighter.

Lynn had dreamed of this day ever since she was a little girl. Her mother had told her to be patient and wait for just the right guy. "It will happen, trust me," Lynn remembered her always saying.

That morning, Ken picked Lynn up for church in his old rusty used Chevelle. It was raining and the car's windshield wipers didn't work, so Ken should have been irritated, but Lynn noticed that he was calmer than normal. "What's wrong with you?" she teased. "Nothing, why do you ask?" Ken replied with a smile.

The rain stopped just as church was over. "Let's drive down by the Mississippi River and check out the water level for my upcoming canoe trip," Ken suggested. "Can't we go back to my apartment so I can change and put on better shoes, I'm in heels Ken," she said. "No, let's just go and wing it," Ken said as he laughed aloud. "You're crazy, but that's why I love you," she said with an endearing look.

The river bank was muddy and Lynn couldn't figure out why Ken was so insistent about checking on the water level. Couldn't he go later by himself, she thought. It was only a few moments later that Lynn knew the answer to her question. As Ken got down on one knee the most wonderful words Lynn would ever hear were spoken. "Will you marry me?" Ken asked. Of course, Lynn said yes as her heels sank further in the river bank mud. "I bought a ring. Do you like it? We can get a bigger diamond as soon as I get a better job," Ken said. "I love this one and will never take it off," Lynn gushed. As they left the river, Lynn was so happy that she almost forgot the sadness she carried. Her mother had died two months before from a long battle with cancer. "Oh Ken, I wish so much that I could just call mom and tell her the good news." "I have a good feeling she already knows," Ken said as they got in the car.

Later that same afternoon, Ken and Lynn took Ken's dog Ralph out to a local park to play Frisbee. "You should take off the ring until we can get it properly sized," Ken suggested. "No way, I promised you I would never take it off," Lynn teased.

HISTORICAL NOTE » Perhaps no other object is as important to a young woman as her diamond engagement ring. It is the one piece of jewelry that every young woman dreams of. Generally made from platinum, gold, or sometimes silver, and usually including diamonds, an engagement ring signifies that a woman is spoken for and engaged to be married.

The ring finger of the left hand is where the ring is usually worn. The engagement ring is representative of a formal agreement between a man and a woman to become married.

The arrangement, or tradition if you will, dates back to ancient times and has a place in history with the ancient Egyptians, Romans, and Greeks. Engagement rings are no longer just for the western civilizations. Brides in almost all cultures have now adopted this tradition.

 TIMELINE 1985

March 6 » Mike Tyson makes his professional debut in Albany, New York, a match which he wins by a first-round knockout.

April 23 » Coca-Cola changes its recipe and releases New Coke.

July 3 » Back to the Future opens in American theatres and ends up being the highest-grossing film of 1985 in the United States.

October 18 » The Nintendo Entertainment System is released in U.S. stores.

Basketball Star

FACTS In order to get some property permissions for metal detecting you have to be willing to share your passion for the hobby with anyone who seems interested. I was presenting a photography program in a small southern Minnesota town a few years ago and after the show an elderly man in attendance told me that he owned a historic house in the nearby town of Wanamingo. Of course, I steered the conversation to my love of metal detecting and soon received permission to hunt his yard. A couple weeks later, I spent an afternoon on his property and wasn't disappointed. Maybe my favorite find at the site was this small 1934 basketball charm.

Stanley Bates couldn't believe his luck that fall. He had walked on as a freshman and made the University basketball team. He knew he wouldn't probably be a starter, but just making the team was good enough.

Basketball had always been Stan's favorite sport in high school even though he also lettered in football and track in the small town of Zumbrota. He was never recruited for a college scholarship, but going to the University of Minnesota and the hope of getting into the School of Engineering was a longtime dream.

Basketball practice and an intense credit load kept Stan so busy that he hardly had time to write to his girlfriend Helen. Helen was a year younger than Stan and was the cheerleading captain for the Zumbrota Cougars. She and Stan had dated for nearly three years. She had plans to follow Stan to the University the next year and maybe study Library Science. When Stan did write to Helen that fall, he always mentioned his new basketball chums and how much fun he was having living in the dormitory on campus. Helen always wrote back right away and kept him up to date with the goings on in their small town.

Years later, Helen would recall the story of Christmas, 1933. "Stanley was invited to our house for Christmas Eve dinner and that is when I recall him telling me, he was going on a basketball trip to California in February. Of course, I was happy for him, if not a bit jealous. Who wouldn't want to get out of Minnesota in February?"

Two months later, Helen came to Minneapolis for the sendoff festivities. The Minnesota Gophers would be taking the train west and play in the Southern California tournament. They had played well all season and now earned a place in the bracket.

"I'll bring you back a souvenir" Stan promised Helen as the team boarded the Chicago and Northwestern. "Just come back to me" she said with tears running down her cheeks.

Sadly, Stan never did make it back to Minnesota and to Helen. During a morning practice before the semifinal game, Stan collapsed on the gym floor from a rare heart condition. The team doctor did all he could, but it wasn't enough. Stan died surrounded by his entire team.

After the funeral in the congregational church in Zumbrota, Stan's coach handed Helen a small box. "Stan would have wanted you to have this," is all he said. Inside the box Helen found a little gold-plated basketball charm. Later, using her pen knife, she carved the initials S.B into the charm. "I will never forget him," she promised herself.

Helen eventually did get her degree in library science, and soon married a local boy from the nearby town of Wanamingo. For years she kept the gold charm in her jewelry box and according to her kids would always tell the story that she once dated a basketball star.

Helen passed away in 1995, and when her children were going through her jewelry the charm was nowhere to be found. ⋄

Small Treasures

May 11 » Dust Bowl: A strong 2-day dust storm removes massive amounts of Great Plains topsoil in one of the worst dust storms of the Dust Bowl.

May 30 » Everglades National Park is established.

October 22 » "Pretty Boy" Floyd is shot and killed by FBI agents near East Liverpool, Ohio.

November 21 » Cole Porter's musical Anything Goes, starring Ethel Merman, premieres in New York City.

Helena Rubinstein   Valaze Makeup Compact

More than a Souvenir

Cleaned

FACTS Many times while metal detecting with friends, you will split the site and each person will work their designated area. If you detect too close to each other, many times the detectors will interfere with each other and not work properly.

Even though it was a rainy day, my friend Steve Olson and I decided to try our luck at a rural permission site near Princeton. When we arrived at the farm, we decided to split the sloping back yard in two halves for the hunt. We agreed that a large oak tree would serve as our dividing line and each of us would scan up to the tree, but not go onto each other's side. At first Steve started finding some older coins and I thought that maybe he got the better half of the yard. All I was digging was trash and old square nails. I decided to move closer to our designated boundary with the hope that my luck would change. Sure enough, right on the imaginary line near the big tree, I got a great signal and pulled up my oldest piece of jewelry (to date). Of course, Steve thought I went over our agreed boundary and found it on his side. "Without an official survey, I said laughing, we will never know".

The brooch dates to the late 19th century in what art historians call the Art Nouveau period. The piece doesn't have a makers mark, but it looks like a design similar to the work of the artist Alphonse Mucha. The beautiful wispy hair flowing on this lovely young woman as she savors the scent of the flower is typical of his work.

Hulda couldn't get off the steam ship fast enough as it docked in Bremen Germany for a short stop. She had been deathly sick from sea sickness in the short two day crossing from Stockholm. All she wanted was to stand on firm ground. "I don't think I can get back on that ship", she told her brother Peter. "You must or we will never get to America. Take some time to walk around the market and I'm sure by tomorrows departure you will feel differently," Peter said with a smile.

Taking her older bothers advice, Hulda was soon distracted by all the souvenir shops that lined the busy wharf. Merchants were yelling to all the new arriving Swedes about the great deals to be had in their shops. It didn't take Hulda long to get drawn into their enticing trap. She knew that she really shouldn't spend any money on souvenirs, but she convinced herself that after almost dying at sea, she deserved something.

"It will look great on you," the German woman shopkeeper said in broken Swedish. The silver brooch image reminded Hulda of her

mothers wedding picture that was in the wood frame back home at her father's farm in Bollstabruk, Sweden. She never knew her mom, for she had died before Hulda turned two. "I will buy this brooch as a reminder of mother," she said aloud. The sales lady only smiled as she put the brooch in a small grey box and handed it to Hulda.

The next day, back aboard the steam ship Germanic, Hulda was excited to show Peter what she had bought. "Doesn't it look like mother?" she asked. Peter stared at the brooch for a long minute and finally spoke. "Yes, from what I remember of her, she had long hair and a beautiful thin face." "Just like my brooch, right?" asked Hulda. "A perfect match," Peter said with a grin. "It feels like I am taking mother with us to America", Hulda said as she put the brooch back into the little grey box. "Maybe just having this with me will make the voyage better," Hulda said. "I sure hope so," Peter said with a bit of sarcasm.

Hulda and Peter did make it to America and years later while living in Minnesota, Hulda met her husband August at a Karmel Covenant church social. They soon married and within a year began raising a family on the farm August had started years before, near Spencer Brook. They had twin girls, Emma and Brita in 1900. Sons John and Carl followed in the next three years, but it was the girls who loved seeing the brooch that Hulda still kept in the same little grey box. Each time she would show it to the girls, she would retell them a story of

their Swedish grandmother. During these story times, each of the girls would take turns holding the silver brooch. Even though they knew the answer, they always asked if they could wear it to school? "I carried it all the way from Germany, Hulda would remind them, and I would be very sad if it was ever lost. It is the only likeness of my mother who I never knew."

Tragically in the spring of 1909 their farm house that August had built with the help of his father, was lost in a fire. A lit kerosene lamp had fallen over and before August could roundup some neighbors to help, the house was fully engulfed in flames. Fortunately, Hulda and the kids were in town that afternoon, but most of their personal belongings were destroyed. Almost immediately, August, with the help of the men from church, began to build a much larger brick house. They chose a spot higher on the hill overlooking the barn and old home site for the new house. Hulda insisted they plant a memorial oak tree on the spot of the old house. "I always want to remember our first home," she would remind the kids.

 1896

January 4 » Utah is admitted as the 45th U.S. state

May 18 » Plessy v. Ferguson: The U.S. Supreme Court introduces the "separate but equal" doctrine and upholds racial segregation.

May 27 » The costliest and third deadliest tornado in U.S. history levels a mile wide swath of downtown St. Louis, Missouri, killing more than 255 and injuring over 1,000 people.

December 25 » John Philip Sousa composes his magnum opus, the "Stars and Stripes Forever".

Cookie Cutter

Lantern

CHAPTER 5

Household

W hy so many spoons? Yes, you find a lot more spoons than you do knives and forks. My theory is that kids used spoons as small shovels to dig in the dirt and left them out in the yard. Although I find a lot of spoons, the one household item I find the most is Mason jar lids. In every farm yard I have ever metal detected, I find them in abundance. I remember the first one I found; I was excited, but now, not so much.

Old Spoons

Mason Jar Lids

The reason household items are found on a regular basis is before weekly trash pickup became the norm, people buried their trash on their property. If it didn't burn, much of the trash items were just tossed in the woods near the house. We don't do that today, but as a metal detectorist, I'm glad they did in the good old days.

Scotty Fork (Bakelite) - 1930's

Stray Cat

FACTS Sometimes while metal detecting you find things that are so random that you have to ask what in world is that doing there? That was the case when I was hunting an old farm site north of Anoka. The signal was strong and I knew it wasn't an old iron nail or Mason jar lid. I pulled this old bell out and was intrigued with the fancy design. The clapper was gone, but I was still happy with the find. It wasn't until I got home and cleaned it up that I noticed a name inside "Sarna".

HISTORICAL NOTE » Bells of Sarna is a brand name used by a company founded by Sajan Singh Sarna in Manhasset, New York. He imported goods from India and sold them to dealers in the United States. Sarna began importing bells in 1938. The bells were often sold on thin ropes or chains and came with a tag that gave the story behind the bell.

The door knocking seemed to go on forever even though Betty tried to sleep through it. She had worked the late shift at the factory making tank parts for the new Sherman. The tank, they were told was going to end the war.

The man at the door was dressed nicely in a pin stripe suit and was carrying a wooden box with a metal strap handle. "Good morning," he said with a smile. Betty tried to be nice, but she would have rather been back in bed. The man said he was selling small decorative bells that came all the way from India. Betty wasn't interested in a bell, but she knew the quickest way back to slumber was to buy one and get this man off her porch.

The next day when Betty was looking at the bell, she thought of a good use for it. She had taken in a large stray cat last month and thought it might be fun to tie it to the cat's collar. With the bell on the cat she could hear it out in the yard and it might give the chipmunks, squirrels, and birds half a chance. She tied it on the collar and waited to see if her plan worked. For the first few days it was a fun experiment, and then one day the cat disappeared and Betty soon forgot all about the bell.

It was years later at her own wedding shower she received a set of Sarna bells as Knick knacks. She couldn't help but smile as she thought about that old stray cat and wondered what had become of it.

 TIMELINE 1943

January 15 » The world's largest office building, The Pentagon, is dedicated in Arlington, Virginia.

February 8 » WWII - Battle of Guadalcanal: United States forces defeat Japanese troops.

March 31 » Rodgers and Hammerstein's Oklahoma! opens on Broadway.

December 4 » The Great Depression officially ends in the United States.

Cowbell

Two Year Job

Before cleaning

After cleaning

FACTS I knew it was a knife, but what kind and how old it was required further research. On a warm day in July, I called an old friend to get permission to metal detect on his property. Al lives between Anoka and St. Francis on a historic farm site that dates back nearly 150 years.

After about a half an hour, I got a signal worth investigating. I was only a few yards from the old barn and wooden silo when this interesting knife came out of the ground. I immediately took it into the house to show Al and ask him if he knew anything about it. Al knows a lot about vintage farm equipment and antiques but couldn't identify the type of knife it was, other than that he thought it was old. The blade is pitted, but amazingly strong. The handle is wood and is attached by three rivets.

Later that night, I posted an image on a metal detecting web site to see if someone could offer some information on the knife. The next day I received a comment from a knife expert who lives in California and he said it was a Green River buffalo skinning knife that dates back to the 1870s or 1880s.

Barn » circa 1883

Lawrence decided there was nothing keeping him in
Minnesota after his father and mother lost most of the farm acreage
in what the newspapers were calling the Panic of 1883. The bank
in Cedar, where Lawrence's folks had banked since arriving from
Scotland in 1865, had just closed its doors as did most of the banks in
area, including the largest in St. Anthony.

Not wanting to burden his parents with another mouth to feed,
Lawrence walked to the train station in Anoka to see if he could sneak
onto a box car and hitch a ride west. Where he was going, he didn't
even know. He figured that maybe going west he could be hired on
with a cattle ranch as a herder. He knew cattle and was a pretty good
rider; all skills he thought would land him a job somewhere.

As the railroad took him further from his home he began to wonder
about his decision. Two days later he was somewhere in Dakota
Territory and he wondered how long his small food stash would last.
Later that day he jumped from the moving train just before it stopped
for water in a small prairie town. It was here he thought he would start
to look for work. As luck would have it, the first person he met in what

Hayes, S.D.

later would be named Hayes, South Dakota, was to be his employer for the next two years.

Bill Nelson was a cattle rancher and large land owner. He had thousands of acres of open range between the Cheyenne and Missouri Rivers and was always looking for skilled cowboys. The job was hard work, but Mr. Nelson paid well and there was always enough food that a man never went hungry. Lawrence worked six days a week and every Saturday would be paid twelve dollars. A fair wage in such desperate times. Sending half of his paycheck home every week was sure to help out his folks and his two younger sisters.

Lawrence learned a lot about cattle and he especially liked branding time and butchering. It got him out of the saddle for a few days which was always a welcome reprieve.

By the time his two-year commitment to Mr. Nelson was up, he had saved some cash and was ready to go back home. The only things he brought back to Minnesota was his bed roll, his favorite saddle, his skinning knife, and two wooden dolls for his sisters that he bought from the variety store in Hayes.

 **TIMELINE 1883**

January 19 » The first electric lighting system employing overhead wires begins service in Roselle, New Jersey (it was built by Thomas Edison).

February 28 » The first vaudeville theater is opened, in Boston, Massachusetts.

May 19 » Buffalo Bill's Wild West Show Debuts In Omaha Nebraska.

May 24 » Brooklyn Bridge is opened to traffic after 13 years of construction.

Vintage Glass

The Peddler

My interest in the lost town of Page, Minnesota goes back many years. I recall meeting an elderly man in Milaca, Minnesota in the 1980s who told me that he was born in the Page hotel. He said the hotel and the entire town is gone. The town used to be on the west bank of the Rum River along the military road, and when the current highway (US Hwy 169) was constructed in the 1920s, the town was bypassed and slowly disappeared.

Recently, I got to know the current owners of the land where the town was located. They agreed to let me do some metal detecting on the site. I was extremely excited to see if I could unearth evidence that might help tell the story of a pioneer river town. Using old newspaper accounts, aerial photos from the 1930s, and the current topography, I began to reconstruct a map of the town on paper. After locating the old road and bridge remains, I could reasonably place the hotel, blacksmith shop, saw mill and other buildings including what the Princeton newspaper from 1902 said, "The Page barn is the largest barn in the country."

Page Hotel

With my metal detector, I immediately began finding farm related relics such as horse and oxen shoes, pieces of old equipment and of course my share of square nails. At first, I was a little disappointed that I wasn't finding personal items such as coins and jewelry. I continued to hunt the area knowing that there must be more treasures to find. I just had to be more persistent and patient.

On my latest hunt, my luck began to change. Two items in particular gave me hope that I needed to continue to work the area and would find more. The first item was a small five-inch aqua green glass medicine bottle with the name Mrs. Winslow's Soothing Syrup. I find a lot of glass bottles when I metal detect because they are near metal objects in the ground. The other relic was the top of a vintage hotel front desk bell. I found both of these items in the area where the Page hotel was built.

HISTORICAL NOTE » Charlotte N. Winslow, a pediatric nurse, originally created Mrs. Winslow's Soothing Syrup as a cure-all for fussy babies. The syrup was first produced in 1849 by her son-in-law, Jeremiah Curtis, and his partner Benjamin Perkins, in Bangor, Maine. It was widely marketed in North America and the United Kingdom.

Mrs. Winslow's Soothing Syrup was known as a patent medication (this term often refers to a product that was marketed in the United States during this time but typically did not prove efficacy or safety). The concoction was used for babies who were crying, teething, or had dysentery, for which the opioid effect of the syrup caused constipation, to treat the diarrhea.

The syrup contained morphine 65 mg per ounce, as well as alcohol. One teaspoonful had the morphine content equivalent to 20 drops of laudanum (opium tincture); and it was recommended that babies 6 months old receive no more than 2-3 drops of laudanum.

One teaspoonful contained enough morphine to kill the average child. Many babies went to sleep after taking the medicine and never woke up again, leading to the syrup's nickname: the baby killer.

At the time, it was generally unknown how dangerous and addictive morphine was, and with the convincing marketing, Mrs. Winslow's Soothing Syrup was very appealing to exhausted caregivers as a cure-all for fussy and teething babies.

Over time, Mrs. Winslow's Soothing Syrup was forced to remove morphine from their formulation, and remove the word 'soothing' from the brand name. Despite these major changes to the recipe and name, as well as the denunciation of the product by the American Medical Association in 1911, the syrup was still sold until the 1930s.

From the front porch of the Page hotel, Martha could see the peddler's wagon coming down the long-sloped hillside on the other side of the Rum River. She knew she had to stand firm against his convincing sales pitch. She secretly hoped he would pass through Page and continue up the road. She and her husband Axel had been operating the hotel for only six months and had yet to make a profit. Axel had left that morning for Onamia to get needed supplies that would be coming from Duluth on the Soo Line Railroad and would be gone overnight. Before leaving, he gave her clear instructions not to buy anything unnecessary and not allow any hotel accommodations on credit. "We need all the cash we can get," he said.

Tom Wilson disliked the name "Peddler". Instead he called himself a Druggist. "I have a cure for whatever you are suffering from," he said to Martha. "I'm not suffering from anything," she said. "Maybe not," Tom said, "but your guests might need a cure and the nearest hospital is a day's ride south to Milaca. Do you ever have any folks staying over that have small children?" Tom asked. Before Martha could answer, Tom took out a small glass bottle from his sample case. He explained that this harmless medicine given in the correct amount to little ones would keep them happy and quiet. "You don't want your other hotel guests complaining of lack of sleep because of a crying baby, do you?" Tom asked. Martha didn't know what to say, since just last week a family traveling through to Brainerd had twin babies and no one got any real sleep that night. She tried to keep families with little kids in rooms away from the other guests, but that wasn't always easy.

Desk Bell

"I'll take two bottles," Martha said. She knew she would have some explaining to do when Axel returned, but Tom sounded convincing. "You won't regret it, Tom said, just have it available for those mothers that just need a break." Martha thought she could keep the bottles under the front counter and tell mothers with babies that they could ring the desk bell and she would give the medicine out on a need basis.

The next day, Axel returned to Page with the supplies and a week's collection of the Duluth Evening Herald newspaper. Before leaving the papers in the hotel lobby for the guests, Martha loved to catch up on world news and the latest fashion reports out of New York. She especially liked politics and President Theodore Roosevelt amused her with his bully style. "I would vote for him," she told Axel, if only women could vote." "It will never happen," Axel teased as he headed out on the hotel porch for an evening smoke.

Scanning the last of the newspapers, Martha noticed a small article on the second to the last page, about Mrs. Winslow's Soothing Syrup. Was that what she bought from Tom yesterday, she asked herself? Curious, she read through the story and to her horror, she learned the truth about Tom's cure-all. Martha quickly went to the hotel front desk and took the two bottles outside. She popped the corks and in frustration, poured out the contents. Still angry, she threw the bottles as far into the weeds as she could. I'll deal with Tom later, she promised herself.

TIMELINE ⟩ 1912

February 14 » Arizona is admitted as the 48th U.S. state.

March 6 » Oreo cookies introduced.

March 12 » The Girl Scouts of the USA are founded by Juliette Gordon Low, in Savannah, Georgia.

April 14-15 » Sinking of the RMS Titanic: RMS Titanic strikes an iceberg in the northern Atlantic Ocean and sinks with the loss of between 1,517 and 1,636 lives.

Silly Spoon

 I find a lot of lost silverware while metal detecting. Knives, Forks and spoons, but mostly spoons.

One warm summer day I was detecting around an old country church south of Elbow Lake, Minnesota and found this New York spoon. As I mentioned, finding spoons is very common, but this one was special.

HISTORICAL NOTE » In 1915, the famous WM Rogers and Son cutlery company began producing a set of forty-seven United States Great Seal spoons (one for each of the states). William Hazen Rogers (born May 13, 1801) was an American master silversmith and a pioneer in the silver-plate industry and whose work and name have survived to the present day. Rogers, together with his two brothers and, later, his son – was responsible for more than 100 patterns of silver and silver-plated cutlery and serving dishes. Many of Roger's designs were influenced by Louis XIV-style patterns of the 17th and 18th century in France, and he was best known for his Elberon pattern and "Presidential" cutlery series. Rogers partnered with other silversmiths at times, and his company and trademarks were eventually taken over by larger companies.

"I just have three more to go and I'll have the whole set," Harriet teased her best friend Cora on the telephone. She and Cora were in the midst of a fun contest to see who could have the complete set of forty-seven spoons first. Cora just laughed nervously as she thought about how this silly contest started in the first place. In the back of Ladies Home Journal magazine, the Rogers Company was promoting their commemorative state spoons. "Get all forty-seven state spoons for just $9.99," the ad read. Each month three more state spoons became available and Harriet and Cora raced to send their money in.

Cora remembered the day when Harriet secretly brought a copy of the Journal to a Women's League meeting at church. As they were looking at the spoon ad, Harriet whispered, "We just have to have them." They had just finished hearing a mini sermon by one of the older church women about the dangers of laying up earthly treasures and were feeling a little guilty about the spoons. "We have to keep it a secret if we're to do this," Cora said, "The older women will think its foolishness and we will never hear the end of it."

It was nearly Christmas when Harriet's last three spoons arrived in the mail, she had ordered two sets. Harriet knew that Cora's husband John had been laid off from his job at the Elbow Lake Creamery and Cora's spoon orders had immediately stopped just three spoons short. Harriet thought it would be fun to surprise Cora at the Women's League party at church with a special Christmas gift.

After the party, Harriet and Cora slipped upstairs to privately exchange gifts. Cora gave Harriet the newest Grace Livingston Hill novel. Harriet was a veracious reader. "Now my turn," Harriet said as she handed Cora her gift. Tears suddenly came to Cora's eyes as he saw the three silver plated spoons. "We tied," Harriet said with a laugh. After a long hug, the two went back downstairs to help the other ladies clean up in the kitchen.

When the night was over Cora's husband John came in the sleigh to pick her up. The roads were all drifted over with snow and their old car would have never made it through. In the haste to not have him wait in the cold, Cora accidently dropped one of her new spoons in the snow. She quickly looked for it but couldn't find it and knew John would be upset and wouldn't understand if she delayed. I'll find it later, she said to herself. John is more important than a silly spoon.

◄ TIMELINE ▷ 1915

January 26 » Rocky Mountain National Park is established.

March 28 » The first Roman Catholic Liturgy is celebrated by Archbishop John Ireland at the newly consecrated Cathedral of Saint Paul in Saint Paul, Minnesota.

May 6 » Babe Ruth hits his first career home run off of Jack Warhop.

May 7 » The RMS Lusitania is sunk on passage from New York to Britain by a German U-boat, killing 1,198.

The Women's Vote

I immediately knew what I had found on that early warm day in May, but would have never guessed I would find four thimbles together. I was hunting behind a small town Catholic Church in central Minnesota when I got a good signal that rang up as a silver coin. In the past I had found a couple of thimbles, but they were both in bad shape. Although these four were flattened together, I knew that if I was careful that I could straighten them. I borrowed pliers from an elderly man who was repairing the wheelchair ramp at the church. I carefully separated the thimbles and using some water cleaned

some of the dirt away so I could read the words. "★Hoover ★Home ★Happiness*" was on each of the thimbles.

In 1928, Presidential candidate Herbert Hoover gave these thimbles out to women to encourage them to come out and vote. It was only eight years before that the United States passed the 19th Amendment giving women the right to vote. Along with thimbles, buttons and pins, Hoover will also be remembered for his unique slogan, "A chicken in every pot and a car in every garage." Hoover won the election by beating New York Governor, Al Smith, the first Roman Catholic candidate for President.

Beverly was getting some awful long stares from nearby parishioners as her twin boys couldn't seem to sit still through Mass. Beverly's husband Richard was on a business trip to Omaha, but when he was home, he always seemed to know what to do when the boys acted up in church. Today Father Conner seemed to be moving slower than usual which only added to Beverly's nervousness. Suddenly she remembered the thimbles in her purse. Maybe they would help keep the boys distracted and quiet for a little while anyway, she thought. To her surprise it worked.

Years before she had even met Richard, Beverly lived in New York and was active in the Suffrage movement. The highlight of her teen years was meeting the activist Alice Paul in a march of protest in Central Park. Beverly knew that the right to vote was getting close and couldn't wait to cast her first ballot for president. In 1920, she placed her mark on the paper ballot for candidate Warren G. Harding. From that day forward, Beverly would always consider herself a Republican. In 1924, she fell in love with Richard and a year later they married and moved to Minnesota. Immediately Richard thought they should join their local Catholic church. He was raised in the faith, but she had never ever been in a Catholic church until her wedding day. Now she and Richard were active members.

Beverly would never forget that warm spring day when she and the twins walked into church. The church was a buzz with hugs and handshakes. "What's going on," Beverly whispered to one of the women standing near the door. "It's so exciting," the lady said. "A Catholic is going to be President, and he's from your home state." Not Al Smith, Beverly thought to herself. "Why the glum look?" the lady asked. "I'll tell you later," Beverly said quietly, "I just have to get through the service."

The week before, Beverly was in Litchfield at a Hoover rally and volunteered to campaign on his behalf. The Democrats hadn't nominated their candidate yet, but Hoover could beat anyone, she thought. We need the women across America to show up at the polls, was the focus of the town rally. Beverly left the rally with Hoover buttons, banners and a bag of aluminum Hoover slogan thimbles.

In the rush to get home from church, Beverly forgot to pick up the handful of thimbles the boys were playing with on the floor at her feet. Later the next day when Fred Beal, the church custodian, was cleaning the sanctuary, he noticed the scattered thimbles and became upset when he saw "Hoover" on them. "Who would ever vote against a Catholic?" he said out loud. Fred took the thimbles outside and flattened them with the heel of his boot. "That'll show them," he yelled to no one in particular. "I think I'll bury them in the parish garden," he said with self-justified contempt.

TIMELINE 1928

March 21)) Charles Lindbergh is presented with the Medal of Honor for his first transatlantic flight.

June 17–18)) Aviator Amelia Earhart becomes the first woman to make a successful transatlantic flight.

July 3)) Scottish inventor John Logie Baird demonstrates the world's first color television transmission in Glasgow.

October 26)) The International Red Cross is formally established.

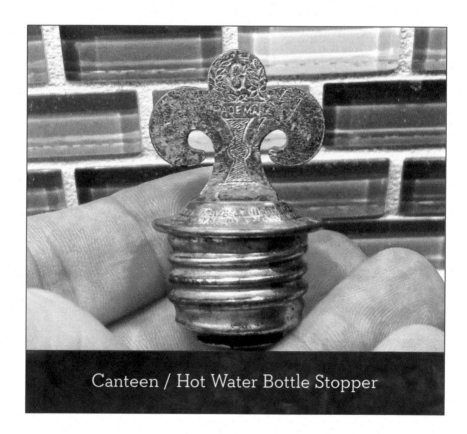

Canteen / Hot Water Bottle Stopper

Comicooky
Baking Set

CHAPTER 6

Military

Metal detecting in Minnesota you don't find a lot of military items, but when you do, it is very exciting. Metal detecting on designated historic battle fields is not allowed without special permission, so I strongly suggest going through the proper channels before detecting. I also suggest that you might want to consider donating any of these finds to a local historical museum, so others can enjoy these wonderful pieces of history.

Navy Button

Strong Sense of Patriotism

Front

Back

FACTS   Sometimes in metal detecting you are surprised beyond explanation. That was the case when I was hunting at a farm site west of Princeton, Minnesota. After about fifteen minutes, I got a clear signal that made me stop and dig. Under a large oak tree in the farm yard, I pulled this Great Seal Button from the First World War.

The land owner's son was following me around as I was detecting and when I found this button, he was more excited than I was. Of course, I wanted to keep the button myself, but when I gave it to him, his expression was priceless. I found out later that he took the button to school to show his high school history teacher and classmates. For that day anyway, he was the center of attention. Sharing history with young people is one of many benefits of metal detecting.

This is the 28mm collectible antiquarian WWI US army 2 part brass metal military uniform Great Seal eagle button. With a press stamped raised relief Great Seal image and the inscription E Pluribus Unum. Great Army Seal buttons have the USA Motto E PLURIBUS UNUM imprinted on them. In 1776 Benjamin Franklin helped to initiate this motto meaning "One out of many", it's probably not a coincidence that in 1902 the US Army began issuing these buttons to any and all enlisted men, from privates to Lt General.

Allen was one of the first boys in line at the Armory in Princeton on that day in April after President Wilson announced America was going to war. Wilson had tried to keep America out of the European conflict, but after several merchant ships were sunk by Germany, he had no choice.

Allen was less than a year out of high school, and was uncertain if he should go to teachers training in St. Cloud or stay on the farm helping his folks. As he began filling out paperwork while waiting for the doctor to give him the mandatory three-minute physical, neither of those career options seemed important to him. His dad had fought in Cuba in 1898, and Allen had always felt a strong sense of patriotism.

After passing all the basic requirements for enlistment, Allen was told to report to St. Cloud on May 1st. His last week at home was difficult as he worked making sure all the farm equipment was ready for spring planting. He knew his dad would have his hands full without him around. Just last year they had purchased the neighbor's farm acreage and were hoping to nearly double the size of their wheat crop. Now with him going into the army, Allen knew his dad would have to let the extra fields go fallow.

Allen's dad and mom drove him to St. Cloud on that rainy May day in 1917. Saying goodbye was the hardest thing Allen could ever remember doing. His mom wept and his dad stood stoically while reaching out his hand as if this was a business meeting. "Come back to us," was the last thing he heard his father say.

Allen served for nearly two years in the US Army National Guard. His last year was in France as a gunner in the famous 42nd Rainbow Division. He would see intense action in July, 1918 in the infamous Battle of the Marne. Although never wounded in action, he would be hospitalized for nearly two months in the fall of that year, due to the flu. It was in a hospital in Belgium that he received a heart wrenching letter from his mom. His dad had a severe farm accident, with one of those new pieces of equipment, which sadly took his life.

After the war and discharge, Allen returned back to the farm outside of Princeton to help his mom. He would always remember his first day home, walking up the driveway seeing his mom hanging out the wash. Her expression on seeing him was sadness and pure joy all wrapped up together. After a long hug and many tears, Allen and his mom sat under the oak tree in the front yard talking about all that happened during the past two years.

HISTORICAL NOTE » US President Woodrow Wilson sought to maintain US neutrality but was ultimately unable to keep the United States out of the war, largely because of escalating German aggression. On May 7, 1915, the Germans sunk the British ocean liner RMS Lusitania, which had over a hundred Americans on board. Wilson warned that the United States would not permit unrestricted submarine warfare or any further violations of international law.

In January 1917, the Germans resumed submarine warfare. A few days after this announcement, the Wilson administration obtained a copy of the Zimmermann Telegram, which urged Mexico to join the war effort on the side of Germany and pledged that in the event of a German victory, the territories of Arizona, Texas, and New Mexico would be stripped from the United States and returned to Mexico. The publication of the Zimmermann Telegram and the escalation of German submarine attacks on US merchant vessels led the US Congress to declare war on Germany on April 6, 1917.

More than 1.3 million men and twenty thousand women enlisted in the armed forces. Though some Americans opposed US entry into the war, many believed they had a civic duty to support the war effort. US government propaganda sought to mobilize the American citizenry through appeals to patriotism and civic duty, and by linking US democracy with support for the democracies of Western Europe.

 TIMELINE 1919

January 1 » Edsel Ford succeeds his father as head of the Ford Motor Company.

January 16 » The 18th Amendment to the United States Constitution, authorizing Prohibition, goes into effect in the United States.

June 4 » Women's rights: The United States Congressapproves the 19th Amendment to the United States Constitution, which would guarantee suffrage to women, and sends it to the states for ratification.

November 10-12 » The first national convention of the American Legion is held in Minneapolis.

.58 Caliber Minié Ball

Camp Cook

THE SIBLEY CAMPAIGN 1863

FACTS I have found many relics and coins during the past several years' metal detecting, but nothing compares to the relics I found at a historic site in North Dakota. My favorite find was a .58 caliber Civil War Minié ball. I also found the grinder from the top of a coffee mill.

My good friend Jay Grammond and I were doing some freestyle photography in North Dakota for a historic article Jay was writing about the "Sibley expedition" of 1863. At a private site near the present town of Binford, North Dakota, we were given permission to take pictures and metal detect.

Coffee Grinder

The site was the location of one of the encampments during the expedition, known as Camp Atchison. It was at this camp site near a small lake that nearly fifteen hundred soldiers spent several weeks waiting the return of Sibley, who was leading a smaller more mobile force went westward.

In the summer of 1863, former Minnesota Governor, Henry Sibley led a large group of soldiers in a retribution campaign against the Dakota Indians. He was ordered to pursue the Indians and push them by force if necessary, west of the Missouri River in what was known then as Dakota Territory. Throughout that hot summer, the soldiers made camp wherever they could find a good source of fresh water. Of all the sites, Camp Atchison was where Sibley's men spent the longest time.

Private Edward Palmer hated that he had been assigned sentry duty on the north wall of the fort. Fort Ridgley faced south and the river and most thought that if there was going to be another attack; it would come from that direction. Edward feared that if the attack came, he would miss out on the action. As it turned out an attack did not occur. The Dakota leader Little Crow, who had led the first two attacks on the fort, had moved his forces further up the Minnesota River.

Growing up in St. Paul Minnesota, Edward had always dreamed of the day when he was old enough to join the army. It was a tradition in the Palmer family. His Grandfather was with General Ripley in the Siege of Fort Erie during the war of 1812 and Edwards's father was also in the army during the Mexican War.

When the Dakota Uprising began in August of 1862, Edward immediately signed up to serve with the Sixth Minnesota volunteers. After two weeks of training at Fort Snelling, he was assigned to Company G. and sent to Fort Ridgley. For the remaining months of 1862 until the following summer, Edward suffered mainly from boredom at the Fort Ridgley. He saw no action and wished his company would be sent south to fight the Confederates. Many of his home town friends in other Minnesota Regiments were writing exciting letters home about places called Shiloh, Antietam and Bull Run. Edward thought the war would be over before he even got a chance to fire his weapon.

In early June, Edward was informed that he would be a part of General Sibley's army of state militia that would move into the Dakota Territories in search of Indians.

Edward became excited as the large column of over four thousand men made its way up the Minnesota River trail. Luckily, Edward was close to the head of the column that stretched over four miles in length. The dust raised by men, horses and oxen made it nearly unbearable for those unlucky ones in the rear of the column. Edward was also lucky that he was chosen to be one of the camp cook assistants in charge of food supplies. With this job, he was allowed to ride in one of the many supply wagons. Most of the enlisted men had to walk, while the officers rode horses.

At each camp site, while the men rested after the long day's march, Edward had to help prepare the evening meals. Scrounging for firewood was his least favorite job. Firewood became scarce as the expedition made its way onto the Dakota prairie. Dried grass and buffalo chips were suitable replacements if necessary. Getting a fire started was always difficult for Edward. He always struggled with this task. One day an older veteran shared with Edward a secret trick to get a good blaze going with little effort. "The trick is to take a .58 caliber Minié ball lead bullet and using a small fork or knife dig out the gun powder and sprinkle it over some dried grass or small twigs. The powder will ignite with the smallest spark. The bullet is useless without powder, so just toss it in the grass. We have cases of those bullets, so no one will even notice." From that point on Edward's struggles with cooking fires were over.

Coffee was the most requested drink if you didn't count whiskey. General Sibley forbade all alcohol so Edward's other major duty was to grind coffee beans. This job using a small hand crank coffee mill kept him busy in the supply wagon for hours each day. The men liked Edward and even gave him a nickname, "The Grinder"

On July 18th the column arrived in the vicinity of a large lake they called Lake Sibley, named after their commander. The camp was named Camp Atchison. Because of a good supply of fresh water and good grazing land, the weaker half of the column was ordered to stay near the lake and rest while the other half of the expedition pursued the Indians westward. Edward was thankful he was assigned to stay at Camp Atchison making fires and grinding coffee.

By the end of the summer, the expedition was back at Fort Snelling and Edwards's dream of going south to fight in the Civil War became a reality. In 1864, sadly Edward died of malaria in the swamps near Helena Arkansas.

Small Fork

HISTORICAL NOTE » By the spring of 1864, the men of the 6th Minnesota successfully argued that they should be sent to the South. They found garrison duty boring and wanted to fight in the war for which they enlisted. Finally, that summer, on June 14, 1864, they left Fort Snelling to go south. The regiment was sent to Helena, Arkansas, where disease began to take its toll. The regiment lost more men to disease than it did in battle. In Arkansas, the regiment observed guerrilla forces in the region but participated in no battles. After a few months, the men were sent to St. Louis and then to New Orleans and then Alabama.

In Alabama, the 6th Minnesota stormed Fort Blakely in one of the last battles of the War. They then guarded Montgomery and waited to be mustered out. The regiment was mustered out in St. Paul, Minnesota, on August 19, 1865.

 TIMELINE 1863

January 1 » President Lincoln issues the second executive order of the Emancipation Proclamation, specifying ten Confederate states in which slaves were to be freed.

January 8 » Ground is broken in Sacramento, California on the construction of the First Transcontinental Railroad in the United States.

July 1 - 3 » American Civil War: Battle of Gettysburg.

October 3 » President Lincoln designates the last Thursday in November as Thanksgiving Day.

It's Only a Button

Front

Back

FACTS Finding military items are always exciting for me, but to find them dating back to the Civil War is extremely rare in Minnesota. I was doing some yard hunting at a house along 7th Avenue in Anoka and found this coat button. At first, I thought it might be a reproduction, but after careful cleaning, inspection and research, I am confident that it dates to the 1860s. It is called an "Indian war' button. It would have come from a soldier's jacket who served in US - Dakota War.

The US-Dakota war was an armed conflict between the United States and several bands of Dakota (also known as the eastern 'Sioux'). It began on August 17, 1862, along the Minnesota River in southwest Minnesota, four years after its admission as a state.

Growing up in the town of Anoka, Billy's favorite holiday of the year was Halloween. He even told his mother that it was more important than Christmas. "Don't be silly," his mother said, "You know it's a pagan holiday, don't you?" Even those kinds of words didn't stop Billy from dreaming every autumn for the one day when he could dress up in costume and eat as much candy as he wanted.

"What should I be this year?" Billy asked his Mother. "Well, you were a ghost last year and a cowboy the year before that, why not a soldier?" his Mother suggested. "I think I have just the costume for you in the attic," she said. She was thinking about that old musty smelling uniform jacket and hat that belonged to her grandfather. I could take it in a little bit and it might be a good fit, she thought.

Halloween finally arrived. Billy could hardly sleep the night before as he was so excited to wear his costume to school. That morning he tried on the jacket to see if it fit, but his mother had altered it too much and now it was too tight. Walking to school, Billy pulled hard on the jacket front to get the buttons to reach and sure enough the middle button popped off. "I'll just get a safety pin from the nurse at school," he said to himself.

Billy won the Washington Elementary school contest for having the most authentic Halloween costume. Before leaving the school for the Halloween parade down Anoka's Main Street, he was asked to tell his fifth-grade class the story behind the uniform. All Billy could remember was that his Great Grandfather was in the war against the Indians and was lucky to not have been scalped. The whole class laughed at the story and Billy almost felt like a war hero himself. "Would you like to ride on the parade float?" Billy's teacher, Mrs. Carter asked. This day could not have been going any better; Billy thought.

That evening after supper, Billy put the uniform jacket back on and was about to join his buddies for Trick-or-treating in the neighborhood, when his Mother noticed the missing button. "What happened?" she asked sternly. "It came off on the way to school this morning," Billy said sheepishly. "Ok, hand it over and I'll quickly sew it back on," his Mother said. "I don't know where it is," Billy said as he began to cry. "Now now boy, stop your crying, it's only a button."

HISTORICAL FACT » In 1920, George Green and other Anoka civic leaders suggested the idea of a giant celebration. The idea was adopted by the Anoka Commercial Club and the Anoka Kiwanis Club; both giving their full support. In September of that year, a Halloween committee was organized.

Working hand in hand were businessmen, teachers from the Anoka public and parochial schools, parents, and students.

For weeks before the big event, more than a thousand Anoka school children made plans and costumes for the big event.

By the 1930s, the festivities had expanded as had the attendance at the parades. There were over 2,000 costumed children marching down Main Street. It was estimated that 20,000 spectators lined the streets to watch this night-time spectacle. In 1937, 12-year-old, Harold Blair, donning a sweater embellished with a Halloween Capital insignia, carried with him to Washington, D.C. a proclamation naming Anoka the Halloween Capital of the World.

 1862

February 1 » Julia Ward Howe's Battle Hymn of the Republic is published for the first time in the Atlantic Monthly.

February 22 » American Civil War: Jefferson Davis is officially inaugurated in Richmond, Virginia, to a 6-year term as president of the Confederate States of America.

May 15 » U.S. President Abraham Lincoln signs a bill into law creating the United States Bureau of Agriculture (later renamed the Department of Agriculture).

July 1 » Taps first sounded in the Union Army.

Steamer Trunk Lock

Dairy Tag

CHAPTER 7

Miscellaneous

This category of items is the relics that don't fit into any of the other groupings. Many times, I find a piece that I have no idea of its origin or even what it is or what it was used for. I call these items, "Mystery finds." On-line research many times helps me identify items in this category.

Pick Axe

Case Closed

FACTS An idea came to me when I learned that Lynne Dablow, the Director of the Isanti County Historical Society, was a trained Archeologist. I asked if she might be interested in working together on a project to recover Isanti County history. She immediately thought it would be a great idea to involve families in an actual archeological dig. She had recently learned about some open property next to the old County Courthouse in Cambridge that was going to be developed. She did some research and found out that there once was an old town school on the site. With city permission, she asked if I would first metal detect the site to see if there were some potential target hits and where the concentration was. I was excited to check the site out with my metal detector.

Although I didn't actually want to dig the signals I was getting, I couldn't resist an amazing hit I got after about an hour on the site. About 8 inches down I found this Opera House tag. Is it a coat check tag or a room key tag? Did the Opera House have rooms to rent?

The Metropolitan Opera House in Minneapolis (320 Marquette Ave.) made its debut in 1894. It was known initially as the New People's Theater but was renamed the Metropolitan just six months later. It was designed by Minneapolis architect Harry G. Carter in the popular Romanesque Revival style. The inside auditorium, which had two balconies and seating for approximately 1,500. According to Historian Larry Millett, the designer neglected to account for a box office, so one was gerry-rigged under a staircase. The Metropolitan Opera House was demolished in September 1937. After serving as a parking lot, the Sheraton Ritz Hotel was built on the site in 1963. The hotel was demolished in 1990, and the site is now the home of the 365 Nicollet apartments.

Throughout the month of December, Carl Swenson had been keeping up with the Minneapolis murder story in the Cambridge Independent. He looked forward to each edition to see what new evidence was being added to the case. He became hooked on the story from the first time he read the following:

> On December 3, 1894, the lifeless body of Miss Catherine "Kitty" Ging was discovered on Excelsior Blvd., just beyond Lake Calhoun in the vicinity of the Minikahda Golf Club. The Minneapolis Journal shouted "Foul Murder!," elaborating that "A Bullet Hole in the Head Tells the Awful Story." Although suspicion fell on her friend Harry T. Hayward, he had an airtight alibi, having been seen at the Minneapolis Opera House on the night of the murder.

Early on in the case, Carl had heard so much about this amazing opera building he had to see it for himself. Inviting his girlfriend Ginger, they caught the train for Minneapolis for a long weekend and two shows at the Opera. Ginger, one of the local Cambridge school teachers, felt safe from the prying eyes of the town's people by going all the way to Minneapolis. Surely, they would never find out. Had it not been for Ginger forgetting to leave the room tag in Minneapolis, her secret would have been safe.

The next Monday, the key tag fell out of Ginger's purse as she was walking into school. Miss. Jones, the head teacher happened to find it in the entry way, and a new scandal was about to erupt in Cambridge. Later that same afternoon, Ginger slipped into Ms. Jones office and took the piece of evidence and after everyone had gone home, she buried it in the school yard. Case closed in Cambridge, but the one in Minneapolis was just going to trial.

Miss Ging, it turned out, had been murdered by the janitor of her Minneapolis apartment building located at 13th and Hennepin. The janitor acted at the behest of Hayward, who did it for Kitty's insurance policies and for the experience of having someone killed. While the janitor drew a life sentence, Hayward swung from the gallows at the Court House on December 11, 1895. In 1911, the death sentence was forever outlawed in Minnesota.

TIMELINE 1895

July 4 » Katharine Lee Bates' lyrics for "America the Beautiful" are first published.

July 6 » Van Cortlandt Golf Course opens in The Bronx as the country's first and oldest public golf course.

September 18 » Booker T. Washington delivers the Atlanta Compromise speech.

November 28 » Chicago Times-Herald race: The first American automobile race in history.

The Lost Tag

FACTS ▷ I found this dog license in a small Park near a wayside historical marker south of Red Wing. I cleaned it up and thought if I called Balsam Lake, the county seat of Polk County, Wisconsin, I might be able to return the tag to the original family. I was excited to see what the reaction might be when I told them that I had their family dog license from 1930.

Unfortunately, the county only keeps records of Dog licenses for eight years. I realized then that it would be impossible to ever find the family.

» The earliest record of a dog license was documented in Utrecht, Holland, in 1446. The fee for the license was paid in pounds of salt.

» There is evidence that dogs were taxed in Germany as early as 1598. One of the oldest known surviving dog licenses dates from 1775 and is from Rostock, Germany.

» The oldest known American dog license tag was dated 1853 issued by the Corporation of Fredericksburg (Virginia).

» During WWII dog license tags were made from pressed fibers because brass and aluminum were needed for making military supplies and ammunitions.

Originally, dog licenses were intended to be disposable and annually renewed. Many have been discarded years ago; however, dog tags are frequently being unearthed through the use of a metal detector. Such discoveries are met with excitement, as even a buried, corroded or damaged tag has value to a collector if it is a rare specimen. Some particularly coveted tags were ornate or sentimental which were kept by the dog's guardian and withstood the passing of time. Dog tags that were mounted on or hung from dog collars were often preserved as a memorial to a very special, beloved family pet.

The windshield wipers couldn't keep up with the torrent of rain. "Watch out," Betty yelled out as her husband George swerved the car to avoid hitting the deer. "I hate driving at night this time of year," George said. "The deer seem to be everywhere." "That wasn't a deer," Betty said, "I think it was a dog."

George pulled over to see if his wife was right and sure enough a brown and white dog was standing in a puddle of water right there along highway 8. After some debate Betty won out and George picked up the shivering dog and put it in the back seat of the Packard. "Tomorrow we can find its owner," George said.

After two weeks of dead-end searching for the dog's owner, including a notice in the Balsam Lake newspaper, George and Betty decided that for the time being they would become dog owners. "Let's name her Apple," Betty suggested. "What kind of name is Apple for a dog?" George responded. "I like that name and that's final," Betty said.

The next day George went to the courthouse in town and registered Apple with the county and was given a small stamped license tag with the number 3192 on it. "Just make sure you securely attach it to your dog's collar. They have a tendency to come off easily," the lady at the courthouse said. "I will," George said with a sigh.

Apple was part Pitbull and had a nose that kept her constantly sniffing for scraps of food or chasing every squirrel in the neighborhood. Betty soon fell in love with Apple and George even began to soften towards the old mutt.

Later that following summer George and Betty made a trip to Lake City, Minnesota to visit Betty's sister June. Apple loved car rides, but this would be her longest one yet. Before arriving in Lake City, George decided to stop at a roadside park near the old town of Frontenac to let Apple do her business and burn some energy before being cooped up in June's small house for the weekend. Putting Apple back in the car after a twenty-minute break, George didn't notice that Apple's license was missing. It was only when they were showing Apple off to June, did they notice the license was gone. George drove back to the wayside park, but was never able to find the lost tag.

 TIMELINE ⟩ 1930

January 13 » The Mickey Mouse comic strip makes its first appearance.

February 18 » Elm Farm Ollie becomes the first cow to fly in an airplane, and also the first cow to be milked in an airplane.

May 15 » Aboard a Boeing tri-motor, Ellen Church becomes the first airline stewardess (the flight was from Oakland, California, to Chicago, Illinois).

July 26 » Charles Creighton and James Hargis leave New York City for Los Angeles on a roundtrip journey, driving 11,555 km using only a reverse gear; the trip lasts the next 42 days.

The Bear

Front

Back

FACTS I'll never forget this hunt, not only because I found a very interesting relic, but because of the heat. In late June, I was given permission to detect on an old farm site near St. Francis. The day turned out to be one of the hottest of the summer. Detecting in extreme heat makes it tough to concentrate and on this day the deer flies were also an added challenge.

I was ready to call it quits when I got a good signal not far from the house. To my surprise this little copper Teddy Bear showed its face for the first time, I suspect, in many years. At first, I didn't know what it was. I thought it was old because of its solid weight and vintage style. I cleaned it up at the farm water pump and showed it to BettyJo who owns the farm. She immediately loved it and asked if she could have it for a small display she was putting together about the history of the farm. Naturally I gave it to her after taking photos of it.

Later, at home I began to do some research. I couldn't say for certain, but I think this was a commemorative piece from Teddy Roosevelt's 1904 Presidential campaign.

HISTORICAL FACTS » The teddy bear is named after U.S. President Theodore "Teddy" Roosevelt.

In 1902, President Roosevelt participated in a bear-hunting trip in Mississippi. While hunting, Roosevelt declared the behavior of the other hunters unsportsmanlike after he refused to kill a bear they had captured.

As news of the hunting trip spread, many newspapers around the country featured political cartoons starring "Teddy" and "the bear."

Meanwhile, in Brooklyn, New York, a shop owner named Morris Michtom saw one of the cartoons and had an idea. Michtom and his wife created plush, stuffed bears and placed them in the front window of their shop.

With permission from Roosevelt, Michtom named the bears "Teddy bears." They were an instant success. Ladies and children carried the bears with them in public. President Roosevelt even used the teddy bear as his mascot when he ran for re-election.

Old farm site near St. Francis

Roosevelt's
1904
Campaign
Button

"I don't want it Daddy!" Hattie cried. "I know it's not a real Teddy Bear sweetie, but they ran out of them before I could buy you one," her dad said with a feeling of sadness.

John had been searching at all the local stores for weeks for the popular Teddy Bear. Ever since, Hattie has seen it in the catalog, she was determined to have one. John had tried all the stores from Cambridge to St. Cloud, but had yet to find Hattie a bear. He even tried to bribe a customer at the Rush Point store who had two bears come in on the weekly delivery from Sears & Roebuck. The man was polite, but said "I have twin girls who would never forgive me if I didn't bring home both bears." On the long wagon trip home from Rush Point on some of the worst roads in the county, John had time to think. He knew that he would vote for Theodore Roosevelt in November, but part of him wished the president would lose, so this whole Teddy Bear thing would go away.

As he neared home, he thought that maybe Mr. Leathers, who owned the store in St. Francis, may by chance have received some Teddy Bears in a shipment of merchandise. "It just might be my lucky day," he said aloud to no one, as he crossed the Rum River on the old iron bridge.

ST FRANCIS MINN.

John had known Art Leathers for years and had always tried to support his friend's business. John arrived just as Art was locking up for the evening. "Wait Art," John shouted from the wagon. Art looked surprised and wondered what John was yelling about. "I need a Teddy Bear, Art; did you get some in today?" "No, John, Art said, but I did get some other campaign stuff with today's delivery. Come on in and I'll show you."

Art reopened the store and led John to the back room to a large wood box. Inside the box were two bundles of American flags, some Roosevelt banners and a smaller box of buttons with Teddy Roosevelt and Charles Fairbanks on them. "We're having a Roosevelt rally in Woodbury Park on Sunday followed by a baseball game at the school," Art said. John didn't care about the rally or baseball; he had other things on his mind. "No Teddy Bears, Art"? "No, I told you that outside", Art said somewhat annoyed. "I'm sorry Art, John said, but you know how Hattie's been since her Mother died. I just can't seem to make her smile anymore and I thought bringing home a Teddy Bear, might do the trick."

"I know it's not the real Teddy Bear doll, Art said, but I noticed in the bottom of the box they added a few of these copper Teddy Bear plates. Take one home for Hattie." "Thanks Art, what do I owe you?" "Nothing my good friend, but on Election Day, make sure you vote for TR."

That November, Roosevelt and Fairbanks won in a landslide and by Christmas every store in the country was selling Teddy Bears and John got his daughter, Hattie the biggest bear he could find. The copper plate bear from Leather's store was never seen again.

TIMELINE 1904

January 12 » Henry Ford sets a new automobile land speed record of 91.37 mph.

May 5 » Pitching against the Philadelphia Athletics, Cy Young of the Boston Americans throws the first perfect game in the modern era of baseball.

July 23 » In St. Louis, Missouri, the ice cream cone is invented during the Louisiana Purchase Exposition.

December 31 » In New York City, the first New Year's Eve celebration is held in Times Square.

CHAPTER 8

Special Hunts

There are some metal detecting sites that mean more than others. Some are personal to me and highlight my continued interest in discovering items that exhibit my own and others' stories.

In the town of St. Francis, Minnesota, I had the chance to hunt a property that was very personal to me. The picture above is a current photograph of the church that my dad built around 1966. The building is no longer a church but the yard is exactly as I remembered it growing up.

It was a warm day in July, but I didn't care about the heat, I was just excited to see if I could find anything that connected my past. After about four hours, sadly I didn't find any definitive relics or items that I could attribute to my life as a kid. I did find a handful of coins that all dated from the 1960's and 70's. I normally don't get that excited about finding coins from this time frame, but these were different. Could it be that some of them were lost by my dad? Maybe the coins were meant for the Sunday school offering, but were lost by us kids during a game of touch football before church.

Home north of Anoka, MN

Another location that I have had the opportunity to hunt was the yard of the house I lived in until I was eight years of age. It is located seven miles north of Anoka, Minnesota. When I knocked on the door and told the current owners that my Dad, Uncles and Grandfather built the house in the early 1960's, they immediately gave me permission to swing my detector anywhere in the yard I wanted to go.

As I walked around both the front and back yards, it was as stroll back in time. The large Oak trees seemed the same as I remembered them. The backyard shed where my Dad raised rabbits was very familiar as if our family had never left.

The first target I detected was a 1968 penny. That was the year we moved away. Was that a sign? I also found a small men's watch. It was in rough shape, but maybe it was my Dad's. I would love to find a picture of him wearing it.

This next location was the house I lived in from age eight to sixteen. My family always called it "The Waco Street house". I received permission from the owners who were the same couple that bought the house from my Mom in 1977.

Waco Street house

I spent an afternoon hunting the entire yard. After getting only a few random hits on the detector, I realized that when I was a kid, we didn't have a lot of money and when we lost a coin or toy, we spent all day looking for it. Funny thing, I did manage to find some coins from the 1960's that we must have missed.

All three of these personal hunts were special for me even though I did not find anything that I would normally even write about. The sites and my personal connection to them made the discovery of relics or coins secondary in importance. The locations themselves were the highlights. I appreciate the current owner's permissions and will always be grateful for the chance to walk the ground that was so much a part of my early life. 🪙

Donald L. Ohman
1929 - 1975

Oldest Relic

If I detect for another twenty years, I will never find an older relic than this Copper Culture knife.

It was late in the season, Steve Olson and I were hunting a farm site in Isanti County, Minnesota. We had hunted most of the morning and we made it back to my truck for a recap of what we had found. I showed Steve this copper piece and said it was junk and was about to toss it into my recycling scrap pail. "Wait a minute, Steve said, you may have a very old knife. In fact, it might be thousands of years old." "Your nuts, I said. How do you know that?" "I've seen them in museums," he said.

Later that day, I sent pictures to two different Archeologists to get their opinion. They both independently verified that it was a Copper Culture knife that may have been made between 4000 BC and 2000 BC. The Old Copper Complex, also known as the Old Copper Culture, refers to the items made by early inhabitants of the Great Lakes region during a period that spans several thousand years and covers several thousand square miles. The most conclusive evidence suggests that native copper was utilized to produce a wide variety of tools beginning in the Middle Archaic period circa 4,000 BC.

Wow! I couldn't believe it. This knife could be older than the Pyramids in Egypt. Crazy thing, I was about to throw it in my recycling bin. Thank you, Steve, for saving an incredible piece of North American history.

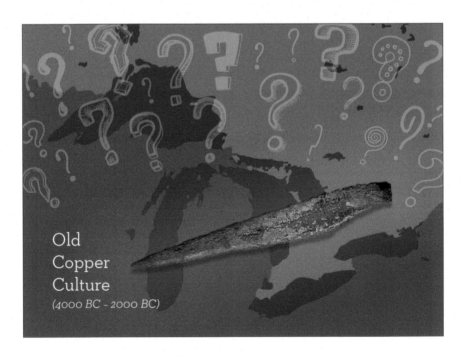

Old
Copper
Culture
(4000 BC - 2000 BC)

The Last Story

If there is one find in the years I have been detecting that stands out as my all-time favorite, it's this one. I was detecting in the woods along a lake shore when my metal detector gave me a reading of "gold". This reading is normally not gold, but trash, then I thought, what if it really is gold. I was shocked to see this beautiful class ring about six inches underground. As I wiped the soil away I could clearly see that it was a men's high school class ring. It was from St. Francis High School and the year was 1973. The ring also had the initials "DN" engraved.

I took the ring home and placed it in my display case over the winter and forgot about it. It wasn't until the following spring while scouting for a barn bus tour in the St. Francis area that I met Valerie Arnold. While visiting with her, she mentioned that she had gone to school in St. Francis and had graduated in 1973. I suddenly remembered the ring. Valerie looked through her old yearbook and figured that maybe the ring belonged to her classmate, Dennis Nutter.

I found that Dennis still lived in the area and gave him a call. Dennis confirmed that he had a class ring but thought he lost it shortly after graduation in 1973. I told him the story of where I found it and he became excited at the thought that his long lost ring had been found. The next day I drove to his house to return the ring. As I handed him the ring, the look on his face was priceless. He offered to pay me for the ring, but naturally I said "no the look on your face is payment enough." Dennis told me "I wish mom and dad could see the ring again, they were pretty upset when I had to tell them I lost my expensive class souvenir." With a grin he said "My kids and grandkids will now know the story."

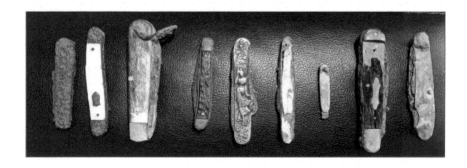

 TIMELINE 1973

January 23 » President Nixon announces that a peace accord has been reached in Vietnam.

February 27 » The American Indian Movement occupies Wounded Knee, South Dakota.

April 3 » The first handheld cellular phone call is made by Martin Cooper in New York City.

October 1 » The Ideal Toy Company debuts the Evel Knievel stunt-cycle, which would go on to become one of the best-selling toys of Christmas 1973.

You just
never
know

CHAPTER 9

Metal Detecting Q&A

Q. Where should I look for lost history?

A. It all starts with research. Using local tools such as historical maps, newspapers, and books will help you determine the best places to metal detect. That being said, there is nothing more valuable in finding the best spots, than talking with local land owners. Many times, they know interesting facts and stories not found in print.

Q. After getting permission to metal detect on private property are there any clues where to begin?

A. Look for places on the property where people may have gathered. Remember, we are looking for historical items that people lost or discarded. I have had success around large old trees, under clotheslines, front yards of old houses, and near mailboxes.

Q. Are there any public areas to metal detect?

A. Yes, but an important rule to follow is to inquire about local laws or rules. Even when a site appears to be open to the public such as park, fair grounds or schools, it is always best to check with local authorities, to ensure you can legally hunt these sites.

Q. Is it hard to get permission on private property?

A. After I approach the land owner with a smile and explain to them that I love history, I will then show them items I have discovered. Most often permission is granted. I carry a calling card with me which helps as well. But let's be honest, not everyone wants people on their land, especially with a shovel. It helps to offer the land owner whatever they want from the hunt. Remember, it's theirs in the first place. After photographing the items, I have given some interesting relics and coins to land owners. It is very satisfying to see their face when I give them a historical relic that connects to their family or home.

Q. Is it expensive to get into the hobby of metal detecting?

A. Short answer is "no." Entry level metal detectors run about $300.00. You can find them cheaper, but you don't want to buy a toy. Most people that participate in this hobby on regular basis have less than $1,000 invested in detector and some basic tools needed.

Q. Where can I buy a metal detector?

A. There are numerous companies that manufacture quality metal detectors. Researching web sites and reading reviews are the best way to begin. If you live in an area that has a local supplier or store, they can be extremely helpful in helping you pick out the equipment you need.

Q. Does it take long to learn how to metal detect?

A. After reading the owner's manual, get outside and try it out. Best place to start is in your own back yard. I found a quarter in the first thirty seconds in my back yard with my first detector. Of course, you will get better the more you do it. It's like golf, practice, practice, practice. Don't forget there is a lot of help out there through YouTube channels, metal detecting clubs and social media sites.

Q. **How far down does the detector go?**

A. This is a very common question people ask me. My best answer depends on a few factors. First, how big is the item that is buried? If it is a small coin such as a dime, you might get a signal at eight inches. If its car door, your detector might pick it up at fourteen inches. Another factor is the type of soil you are detecting in. I find sand is easier than clay for deeper targets. Lastly, moist soil gives you better depth with most detectors. I like to go detecting after a rain storm.

Q. **Are there any risks in metal detecting?**

A. Yes, there are a number of things to be aware of when metal detecting. Be careful of electrical, gas and phone lines. The invisible fence for dogs can easily be cut if you are not careful. In yards or ball fields, watch for sprinkler systems located just under the surface. In the woods, watch for Poison Ivy, Oak and Sumac. Lastly, the family dog might not know you have permission.

Typical Hunt

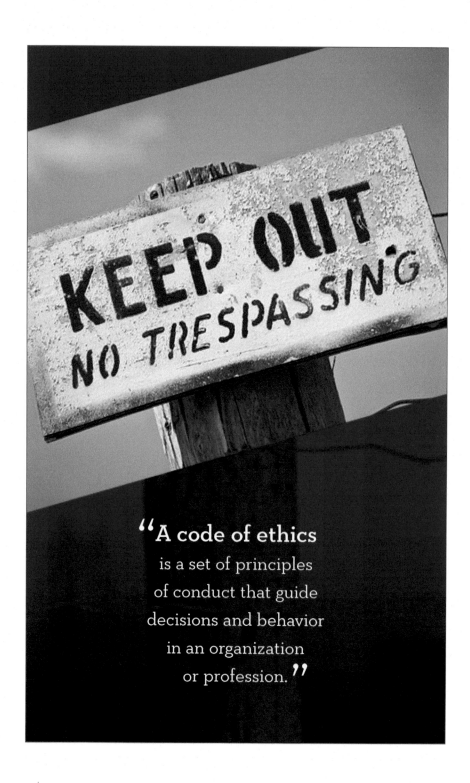

"A code of ethics is a set of principles of conduct that guide decisions and behavior in an organization or profession."

CHAPTER 10

Code of Ethics

P lease be a good ambassador for the hobby and make it easier on yourself and other detectorists to get new permissions, by following these basic ethics for respecting nature, history and property owner.

I **will** respect private property and will not metal detect without the owner's permission.

I **will** not destroy property or buildings.

I **will** never litter, always pack out what I take in, and remove and recycle all trash found.

I **will** leave all gates and other accesses to land as found.

I **will** not damage natural resources.

I **will** abide by all laws, ordinances, or regulations that may govern my search

I **will** fill all plugs and never dig in a way that will permanently damage vegetation.

I **will** report the discovery of items of significant historical value to a local historian or museum.

I **will** be a positive ambassador for the metal detecting hobby.

CHAPTER 11

Added Benefits

O n occasion I have had the opportunity to share my love of metal detecting with young people. Most kids are naturally curious and not shy about asking what I am doing when they see me detecting. When I show them what I have found, they get excited and want to help me find more treasure. I also enjoy sharing with older folks as well. It is a hobby that reaches all generations. I always see this as an opportunity to show kindness and also pass on my love of history with them. Here are some real life photos.

My friends Carl and Phillis

Friends hunting together near Howard Lake, MN

Another added benefit to metal detecting is what my friend Steve Olson does with some of the relics he finds. He turns them into fine art, jewelry and vintage household decor. Here is just one example of what he made from a piece of scrap decorative brass. 💍

Scout Slide

Boy Scout Hatchet

CHAPTER 12

Additional Finds

Civil War Minié Ball

1909 S VDB

Canadian Penny

Japanese Yen

Mazuma Token

Token

1788 Spanish Reale

"Keys, keys... where are the keys?"

Steve and Luke

St. Paul City Railway Co. Token

Silver Ring

Avon Lipstick

Early Season Hunt

CHAPTER 13

Conclusion

There is a British Television program that I like. The show is called Detectorists and in the final episode I loved what was said. "Metal detecting is the closest you will get to time travel. We unearth the scattered memories, find the stories and fill in the personality". That is what I hope I have done. Thank you for taking the time to read the stories and learn more about metal detecting. My hope is that it has been enjoyable and informative.

Late Season Hunt

Excited? Yes!

CHAPTER 14

Acknowledgements

There are a lot of people that have supported me in my hobby of metal detecting and I want to acknowledge them here. First of all this hobby would not be possible without the permission of landowners and caretakers. I have received their permissions with a thankful heart. I mainly metal detect by myself, but on occasion, I go with friends and family. A big thank you goes out to Steve Olson and Jay Grammond for being my hunting buddies.

I was with Jay when I found my first metal object. For most people it is nothing to get excited about, but that old scrap of barbed wire started it all for me.

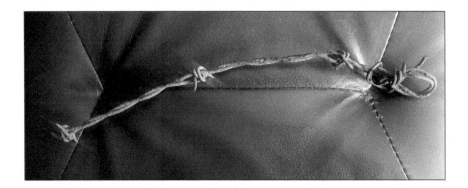

Thanks to my brother Dan Ohman for coming along on numerous hunts. His love of history has made for many fun afternoons in the field. Thanks to all my Facebook friends who give me tons of support when I post pictures of my finds on-line. I appreciate those who read these stories and gave me helpful suggestions. Your advice was very helpful. I have saved the best for last. My sweet wife Krin has been my biggest fan and support. Even when I bring dirt into the house, she gives me that look, but always with a smile. 🜨

Thank you.

Notes

Notes

Notes

Notes

Notes

Notes

Notes